I0445806

Finally Home

Bienvenue Press

Published by Bienvenue Press, 2019.

This is a work of fiction. Similarities to real people, places, or events are entirely coincidental.

FINALLY HOME

First edition. November 29, 2019.

Copyright © 2019 Bienvenue Press.

ISBN: 978-0578618173

Written by Bienvenue Press.

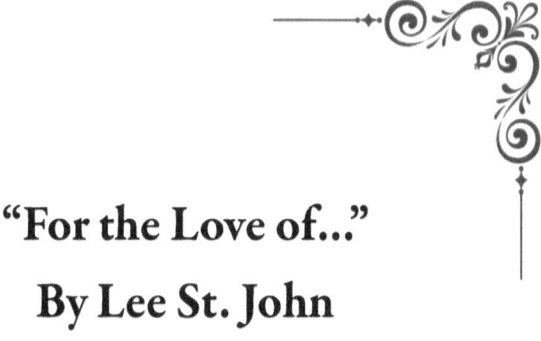

"For the Love of..."
By Lee St. John

My head hurt from crying, my eyes were bloodshot, and I was emotionally drained. But once we left, I said, "It's taken us a long time to get you. Let's go home." *Twice.*

Of course, I'm talking about adoption. Are you an adoptive parent? I am not talking about just fur-baby adoptions. The whole adopting process is emotional. Heart-wrenching. Unpredictable. Uncertain. Hopeful. Your heart is full of love before you even know the angel that will finally be yours.

I am supposed to write about a love story. And this is a love story times two.

As an only child with parents who were forty when I was born, it was lonesome growing up. However, even though I was lonely, I learned how to keep myself entertained. But if you are like most only-children, you often wish you knew what 'the other side' living with siblings was like.

Pets took the place of having an entertaining sibling, in some ways, I suppose, but growing up, my previous pets were also strictly 'outside dogs" as we lived in the country and they were never considered 'a part of the family' enough to live under our roof. When I married, my husband's family pampered their pets because they were purebred and 'deserved' to be respected. Well, think about it...their expense was one way they put a value on their respect. So, because my husband was used to having an indoor dog, we purchased a couple, Bonnie and Oliver. When I say purchased, I mean, those expensive, 1950s popular, and prior Westminster Best in Show winner – the Sealyham terrier .

Oliver was bred in the foothills of Appalachia in North Georgia and Bonnie flew in from a breeder in Ohio. They were my love-bugs before I had my own children. They certainly entertained me and I, them. When I arrived home from work and hubby was either out of town on business or hadn't arrived home yet, the dogs and I had a playfully grand time.

Hating to admit this and never letting it go on too long, I'd sometimes, but rarely blindfold them both and call them from another room to check their hearing. *Playfully*! I'd also sometimes lined my fur babies up with Oliver's foot on Bonnie's hot spot and when I scratched his hot spot, he'd scratch her hot spot, and it was hilarious. Come on! Don't tell me dogs don't have a sense of humor. Now, don't you worry. I wasn't a masochist or anything. I genuinely loved my babies and played with them like a child played with dolls, I guess. They knew I meant no harm.

After their old-age passing, we had another male Sealyham terrier, who we named Teddy. Our oldest son was in upper elementary school, our youngest was around three, and I was teaching middle school. I loved those students and began a campaign with them to "Help Name Our Dog". Theodore was my family's favorite of the proffered names and of course it was shortened to Teddy.

Teddy was schizophrenic (by that I mean he loved and protected my husband, but was only barely tolerant of me). I stayed clear of him because as adorable as he looked on the outside, his brain was scrambled. We thought at the time he might have been the product of "too much inbreeding". He would wag his tail while being petted by a new acquaintance but yet be growling and baring his teeth a bit. It was scary to think he might chomp at any moment. He didn't and we survived him.

After Teddy passed over the rainbow bridge and having raised these previous terriers from puppies, we tried our hand at rescue. With the Sealyhams becoming more rare, which also meant getting more and more expensive, they were becoming financially out of our league. There was a Scottish terrier rescue in the area and we just felt compelled to give it a go. We loved terriers and we (I) thought a scotty would work well for us. And our scotty, which we named Scotty, did. But he died from cancer pretty soon after he moved in.

Sad to lose our sweet boy, we (I) researched another terrier who was supposed to be the perfect pet for children and concluded the best match was a Soft-Coated Wheaten terrier: the perfect playful house pet. This breed's personality stayed puppy-like longer than most other terriers. And because my household was full of too much testosterone, we (I) wanted a girl because it had been a while since we had one, and we (I) felt it was my turn again.

They say do not buy a dog from a retail pet store. However, luck must have been on our side because we purchased the sweetest girl in the world (to pacify me) and at a discount (to pacify my accountant husband). And here is where my great love for this girl started.

All the other pets, as darling as they were, really belonged to my husband. Whereas I was busy raising our children, as much as I adored our pets, I was just not as attached to them as my husband. *He* was the one who chose the breed for our family because of his family's attachment; *he* was the one who took care of their needs as I was busy taking care of our young boys; *he* was the one who went with our oldest son to dog shows so our Sealyhams could obtain their Best in Breed accolades...it was all him. And so he should have had first choice.

But when the boys were busy with their school functions and I wanted a companion at home...I wanted that female. And so along came Kelly...just at the right time. My mother had passed and I needed a female family member. I was left with a house full of hormonal boys and a bull-in-a-china-shop husband. Didn't I get a turn? Kelly saved me during those immediate crying years from the of loss of my mother. I pretended like she was a sister I never had.

She lived with us for thirteen years. The longest of any of our pets, and I was devastated when she left us. She was all mine. Sure she was the family pet and loved all of us, but she was my sidekick, my female confidant, and my constant shadow.

My husband said, "Let's take a break for a while from pets." We still had a cat and he (see...*he*) satisfied like cats do. Hubby wanted to be able to travel and do a few things without worrying about a dog. He knew I was heartbroken about Kelly. Maybe he wanted me to heal before we might try to open our hearts again.

Two years passed and I was again lonely. Our boys were grown and I didn't have a baby to dote on anymore. When finally I just started peeking...just little peeks...on sites for pet adoptions. My computer mouse always clicked on the white dogs, the medium-to-small dogs, the ones with terrier beards and curly fur. One day, there was the face I couldn't ignore and it was available! It was a perfect choice for us and we signed up on-line, ran up to North Georgia's Kennesaw's Pet Smart on the day that Mostly Mutts was setting up pets for adoption.

We got there early. Ran up to be first in line but was told although we qualified with our paperwork, we were second in line to have a shot at bringing this darling boy home. Someone had gotten their paperwork in first and although they were not there for pick up for their designated time, we would have to wait a bit to see if they were going to show up.

This precious schnauzer had a roller coaster life so far, it seemed. Loved by his first owner, who died, her children took in her two dogs. Having five dogs of their own and several children to boot, this proved too much for their family. They had to make the tough decision to find the matriarch's pets a new forever home.

Hearing the news of waiting to find out if this dog who needed a home like ours was going to actually be ours was agony. It brought back memories of another adoption in 1993.

With our firstborn arriving in 1985 after just one month of attempting to get pregnant, we assumed there would be no problem getting pregnant again. Boy, did God have other plans for us. With preparing myself for a second go-round three years later, my yearly gynecological exam found a cyst the size of an orange on my right ovary. With surgery scheduled to remove it, the medical experts determined it to be the size of a grapefruit and needed to remove this larger mass. Doing so, a part of my right ovary was also removed. That ovary must have been the one that was doing its job because for the next five years, even with hormonal treatment to perpetuate more eggs for fertilization, those were never on my right ovary. And for some reason my left ovary was producing eggs but they never took the bait.

I am an only child, remember. I wanted more than one baby. So we turned to adoption, which if you have ever tried to adopt you well know it is a nightmare. For the next five years until our second son's arrival, we tried synthetic hormonal producing drugs to increase the chances; we applied to reputable adoption agencies to put ourselves on their lists after filling out multitudes of forms (this was in the late 1980s and there we no forms online – they all had to be filled out by hand); I duplicated those forms and handed them out to every high school counselor, every attorney, every hospital's delivery wing staff, every gynecologist, and every hairdresser in my area (are you thinking about why a hairdresser? Because they listen to customers talk and they know *a lot*! – Makes sense right?)

I did all the legwork in getting the information out there about how we were looking to adopt. Several became available and then fell through at the last minute. That's tough. You think it might happen and you start to decorate a nursery and then your world falls apart as the birth mother changes her mind for various reasons. I started getting used to that scenario and becoming depressed. I loved one child and knew what that felt like. I wanted to complete my family with four of us.

Then it happened. After years of disappointments, we finally were blessed. We were chosen. But again the event was a heavenly nightmare. Although a Florida adoption, the twenty-year-old birth father lived in Rhode Island and did not have legal representation. Our Georgia attorney who was working with a Florida attorney representing the birth mother had to instruct him and hold his hand from afar in every move to sign away his rights. It was a tough situation for all concerned. The young man didn't move fast enough and what should have taken about three days turned into a week.

And we waited.

Here I was again at the Kennesaw, Georgia's Pet Smart...waiting. All the emotion of the adoption of our son, all the delays, all the effort, all the ups and downs and stops and starts of those years waiting to see if it would happen ... waiting to know the outcome came flooding back. I bust out crying. Right there in the dog section.

The person in charge of adoptions was taken aback, of course, and I had to explain how unsure we were if taking this precious pup home with us was going to take place, just like in my uncertain past experience of adopting our youngest child. I just couldn't help my emotions from taking over.

Maybe that and the fact that the first family at the top of their list never showed within the half-hour of their designated time, we were given our gift and not long after signing all their paperwork, we were finally home.

And we were blessed again and that made *twice*.

About the Author

As a storyteller, Lee St. John has been compared to family funny woman Erma Bombeck, but with an edge; Southern humorist, Lewis Grizzard, but with PG-13 rated twists; genuine tell-all, Ali Wentworth, fearlessly describing her secrets; and any frisky *Seinfeld* episode—especially when George is involved. Betcha thought she'd say Elaine. Since high school, she has had her own newspaper columns and was told once by a publisher she should write a book. Majoring in journalism and mass communications, her first job after college graduation was with a national advertising agency. Think *Mad Men*. Later attending graduate school in English education, she taught every grade but first. A Georgia Peach, Lee St. John has been married to her Southern gentleman for 35 years. They have two Millennial sons and a tater-tot-looking Schnauzer, OBie.

Facebook: https://www.facebook.com/leestjohnauthor
Instagram: https://instagram.com/leestjohnauthor/[1]
Website and Blog: http://www.leestjohnauthor.com
Twitter: @LeeStJohnauthor[2]

---

1.   https://instagram.com/leestjohnauthor/%20

2.   http://www.twitter.com/LeeStJohnauthor

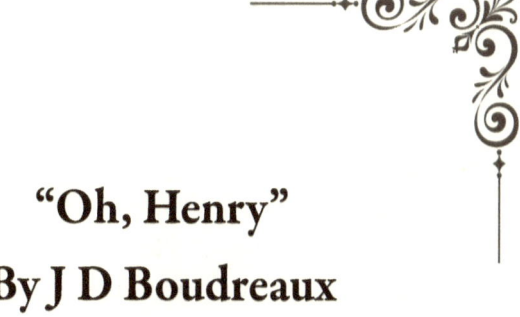

"Oh, Henry"
By J D Boudreaux

OLIVE WALKED OVER TO where Henry was sitting and staring intently at the newspaper.

"Whatcha doin'?" she purred, leaning against his right side.

"Looking at this ad," Henry half-growled. It wasn't an indication of anger at Olive, though she could certainly raise his hackles on occasion.

"What's it about?"

"There's this new anthology that's going to be published by Bienvenue Press."

"Really?"

"Yeah, my dad's been at his computer a lot lately."

"My mom, too." Olive sat on the arm of the sofa, stretching her back. "Think they've been working on another story?"

"They are writers."

"That's how they met after all."

"And indirectly how we met."

Extending her arm playfully, Olive added, "Who could ever forget?"

"I'd like to," Henry muttered to himself.

"Personally, I think we could come up with a good story. Well, *I* certainly could."

"Sure, Olive," Henry yawned. "What could you possibly write about?"

"Maybe a *little ditty about Jack and Diane...*"

"Quit your caterwauling." Henry warned Olive with a sideways glance. "You and your mom listen to way too much '80s music."

"Careful, Henry," hissed Olive. "You might find yourself having *eyes without a face.*"

That did raise Henry's hackles, and he growled back. "Might be a better choice than seeing your fat butt in front of my face while I'm trying to sleep."

Olive extended her nails in Henry's direction, but her attention went back to the newspaper advertisement. Something caught her eye, and she hopped off the sofa.

"Henry. Read that ad again."

Henry remained motionless.

"Henry! Look!" Olive was insistent. "It's about rescue animals? And look at all the hearts? Are you thinking what I'm thinking?"

"God, I hope not."

"Loooove," Olive purred again while practically prancing in front of Henry. "I think I know what they might be writing about. It's what I'd write about. Us!"

"Whoa... not about us. We fight like cats and dogs."

"Oh, Henry...we are a cat and a dog."

TWO YEARS AGO

"COME ON IN, HANK." Christine backed away from the doorway and allowed him and his French Bulldog to enter.

"Just let me put this old boy outside," came the reply as both went striding right past her. "I really appreciate you letting me bring him over again."

The first time Christine had agreed to let Hank bring his dog, she had assumed that he would be kept on a leash. Her yard did not have an enclosed fence or a gate to keep him contained. When she had warned Hank, he smiled and replied, "No worries. He's well-trained... and a little bit lazy. Aren't you, Henry?"

That name!

Christine was still in disbelief that a guy named Hank named his dog Henry. She had to restrain herself from rolling her eyes again as she also wondered why she had ever agreed to this assignment.

Back inside the house, Hank rubbed his hands together and smiled at her. "Ready to make some money?"

Oh, yeah. That's why.

Both Christine and Hank were freelance writers. That's all Hank did. He took one assignment after another from whomever and whatever. She, on the other hand, was in need of more stable employment. She'd lost her last job with the local newspaper when it was sold to a huge conglomerate. The newspaper still existed, and she called the latest version of the local rag *The Copy & Paste.*

Ninety-nine percent of their articles were lifted from the wire service or from the newspaper in the nearby larger city. That paper was also owned by the same conglomerate, and only rarely did they send one of their journalists—if you could even call them that—down from on high to cover any local event.

Dial the number listed for the newspaper these days, and instead of an extensive menu, you only get Option 1, Classifieds; and Option 2, Circulation. In other words, if you have money, they'll take your call.

Christine had landed her current assignment when she responded to an online post seeking writers for an upcoming anthology. The collection would contain stories about living in a small town. Desperate for money if not a real job, she had sent in an inquiry along with a sample of her writing and had received a reply the following week. She had been accepted, but there was one stipulation. She had been paired with another writer who had just moved to her town earlier in the year. That writer was Hank, a "Big City" boy from a suburb of Chicago.

The publishers of the anthology thought it would be an "intriguing and delightful" idea to have a woman and a man collaborate and share their unique views from the perspectives of a native and a newcomer.

Infuriating and despicable were the words that came to Christine's mind when she received the news. That opinion didn't change much once she had met Hank.

He was a nice enough guy, and an excellent writer and researcher, but at times, he was just as goofy as that mutt he brought over.

"We should be ready to send everything off for the initial edits by the end of the week," Christine said. *Time to get this mess finished and Hank out of my life.*

"Guess we should put our collective noses to the grind-stone," replied Hank.

Lord, he did not just say that. I swear he's Bartlett's for Dummies.

On her way to the kitchen to retrieve the pot of freshly brewed coffee, she rolled her eyes and wondered if ten thirty in the morning was too early for Irish coffee.

Near the doorway was a bookshelf. Eye-level was her stereo receiver. She pressed the round button, causing it to glow lime-green, and music flowed through her surround sound speakers.

The song, "Maneater," by Hall & Oates filled the room.

Christine grinned.

MY ORIGINAL PLAN WAS to return this evening, under the cover of darkness. The empty feeling in the pit of my stomach vetoed that plan. I wasn't sure if I could last until noon, much less nightfall. Luckily, the owner of the home was a young woman. Skinny. Not likely to be a serious threat as far as I was concerned.

"You won't find much in there."

I wasn't scared to hear someone behind me. I made it a habit to keep my senses sharp and to never reveal any emotion. "Never let them see you sweat" had become my mantra ever since I'd heard that deodorant commercial blaring from the outdoor television of the sports pub as I picked at the last shred of meat from an abandoned order of chicken wings.

Before entering the yard, I had done a quick reconnaissance of the premises. If things took a turn for the worse, my escape route was already mapped out. Jump on the trash can to create a distraction, over the picnic table as an obstacle, and clamber up the garden trellis to get over the fence.

"She's a vegan." The voice was closer and sounded oddly garbled. "I think she's a vegan. Or was it a Virgo? To tell you the truth, I'm not really sure."

I slowly turned to see who was behind me, and I could not believe this oaf. He was actually chewing on a plastic straw, thus explaining his bewildering speech impediment. If anyone can be as stupid as he looks, then this would be the guy. Still, I moved so that we were face to face, the trash can still a foot or two away.

I used my usual confident and unconcerned voice. "Vegan or not, I'm not choosy."

"Suit yourself. I'll take the usual smorgasbord back home."

Smorgasbord? Where would this dumb wag learn a word like that? But on the other hand, if he had access to such...

"Really?" I was still playing it casual, but I put a little flirtatious lilt to my tone. "And where is 'back home,' if I may ask?"

"Couple of blocks that way," he answered looking to his left. Then he turned to the right. "Or is it that way?"

"You don't know?"

He scratched at his ear way longer than necessary. "I always get distracted on my way over here."

"Then how exactly do you get here?"

"My dad."

"Your dad?"

"Well, he's not my real dad. He adopted me."

I looked to the heavens and asked God to please explain what I had gotten myself into.

"My name's Henry."

Like I cared.

"Are you homeless?" Henry asked me.

The nerve! "I prefer to be called 'feral,' thank you very much."

"Only because you've never had a home before."

As I sniffed around, I realized the doofus was right.

"I make do." I noticed any trace of authenticity was clearly lacking in my voice.

My nose twitched, trying to decipher if any meal from a garbage receptacle would be worth my while. That's if I could even get the lid open. These square plastic Waste Management containers were difficult to get into. I once saw an old movie with round metal trash cans. So easy to knock over and raid. What ever happened to those? Made me wish I lived in the '80s.

But I didn't. To survive nowadays one had to adapt, and I was quickly mastering my craft. I just needed to find the right amount of leverage.

"You're probably wasting your time."

"I hope not..." He was breaking my concentration.

"When's the last time you ate?" he asked.

It was no use. I wasn't going to figure out a way to open that lid with Henry the Harasser buzzing in my ear like a flea.

"Can't remember," I answered, even though I did. "Maybe a corner piece of a Pop-Tart that fell to the ground when some kid got on a school bus yesterday morning."

"I love Pop-Tarts. All that sweet gooey-ness inside."

I swear Henry was practically drooling, but my own mouth was beginning to water at the memory of that pastry piece. I didn't have much room to disagree, did I?

"What flavor was it?" he asked. "Cherry? Brown sugar and cinnamon? That's my favorite."

"I have no idea. It wasn't a big enough piece to have any filling."

"That's all you ate? That's not a meal; that's a crumb."

"I'm not finicky."

My words made Henry laugh. In a moment, I did, too.

"I've been surviving on water mostly." Not always the cleanest water, but no way was I telling him that. The fact was, I was currently on a diet that would make a supermodel jealous.

"A girl's gotta watch her figure, right?"

"Huh?" Henry scratched his ear again.

Oh, brother.

I watched him approach the trash container, sniffing it as he walked around. Henry was bigger than I was. Certainly stronger. Maybe he knew a way in. Was he thinking the same thing I was?

"Kale. Expired cottage cheese." Henry was not pleased. "No, we gotta get you something better to eat."

Distracted by hunger, I bumped into an arrangement of mums.

"Are you okay, my friend?"

Friend?

"You seem a little, I don't know... off? Weak?"

Hello, Captain Obvious!

I said nothing, however, following him off of the concrete driveway and onto the lawn. We settled in the shade under the picnic table. I stretched out upon the ground and closed my eyes.

"All right," I confessed. "Yes, I guess you could consider me homeless, but if I never had a home to start..."

"Really?"

"No. I've always been on my own."

"Wow." Henry laid on the ground. "That's sad."

Okay. That did it. It was time for me to move on. Hungry or not, I wasn't sticking around and listening to this fathead. I didn't have much, but I had my stubborn pride. "I don't want or need your pity."

I was halfway down the driveway, when the door of the house opened, and a woman and a man stepped outside. The skinny woman I recognized. From my reconnaissance missions the previous day, I knew she was the owner of the house. The man, I assumed, was Henry's dad.

Speaking of which, I heard Henry's lumbering footsteps behind me, and him calling out my name.

Unnoticed before, that's when I spotted the vehicle coming up the driveway.

I was trapped! Car in front of me; Henry behind me. The man and woman to my right; a tall wooden fence to my left. Even at my best, I could have never jumped that fence without something to assist me. The garbage container, picnic table, and trellis were all too far behind me now.

All I could do was stare at the grille of the car baring down on me. Henry called out my name one last time before I went sailing through the air and my world faded to black.

CHRISTINE AND HANK sat next to each other on the worn sofa in the waiting room.

She noticed Hank's forlorn, hangdog expression, as he filled out the paperwork on the clipboard provided. Despite her prickly nature, Hank had never been anything but nice to her. In her small town, small-minded way, she'd always viewed Hank as an outsider and an intruder. Especially the latter, since she had no choice but to share the byline with Hank. At least she didn't have to share the money, she'd thought, since the publishers were paying each the full promised and advertised compensation.

So many past thoughts came to Christine as she sat there with Hank, and she was embarrassed. He'd asked her a million questions about his new city, her hometown, and she'd been annoyed by each and every one. She'd been so selfish. Had she ever asked him a question about his hometown, or any question at all that had shown any interest in him or his life?

Her eyes followed as Hank returned to the desk and tapped on the frosted glass window. She also watched as the receptionist took the clipboard from his hand, listening to Hank's question before shaking her head. A dejected Hank returned and sat in the chair along the opposite wall instead of the sofa next to her like before.

The way she was feeling, she didn't like herself either. But she knew that was not the real reason he'd sat elsewhere. He'd chosen a seat where she couldn't easily see his face. She was all but certain that water was welling up in his eyes.

"No word about Henry?"

It took a moment, and Christine was about to let it drop, giving Hank his needed peace and quiet. Even when Hank spoke, she wasn't sure he was really speaking to her.

In a voice barely audible, Hank said, "I don't know what I'll do without Henry."

It tore Christine's heart apart, and she rose from her seat and approached Hank. Placing a hand on the arm of his chair, she tried to comfort him.

"Henry is going to be fine."

If nothing else, Henry was as solid as they come. Stepping onto the patio to await the pizza delivery, Christine had just enough time to see Hank's dog chasing that strange cat. In the blink of an eye, the car's bumper valance missed the cat and hit Henry. The poor thing bounced off of the car before tumbling a few times across the concrete of the driveway. It was almost comical if it wasn't such a serious situation. Landing on his feet, Henry attempted to take one step and fell down. When Henry didn't get up, she and Hank ran to him.

The shock that she had seen on Hank's face also contained concern. When she noticed Henry was breathing normally and the odd angle of one leg, she was relieved. Not that the injury wasn't serious, but for a second she was sure that Hank would have given CPR and probably mouth-to-mouth to his dog, if the situation called for it.

"He's all I got," Hank said, his head in his hands.

Christine pulled the adjacent chair and turned it. Sitting directly across, she waited until Hank's face lifted and met her gaze.

"So... what's your story... with Henry?" she asked.

Hank's expression changed. She should have known a long time ago that Henry was Hank's favorite topic of conversation.

"I got him the first day I moved to town. I had stopped at the Fill-a-Sack, the one by the Chelsi Towers. The animal shelter was having their Pet Adoption Day, and I asked myself, 'Why not?' Didn't have any friends here in town yet, might as well start with one who'll basically love you back, right?"

I wouldn't doubt that Henry loves you as much as you love him, Christine thought.

"Why Henry?" she asked. "I mean specifically him and not some other dog or animal."

"I always loved dogs. Used to have one when I was a kid. But why Henry? He was different. I think even you see that."

"I do." *If different meant odd and goofy... and utterly devoted.*

"Now that you ask," Hank added thoughtfully, "I really think it might be because he reminded me of me."

Christine did her best to keep a straight face as Hank scratched behind his right ear.

"Other dogs would jump and bark and go crazy if you went near their pen," Hank continued. "They wanted to grab your attention. Henry just sat and watched silently. He took everything in. If someone approached him, he would stand, as if out of respect. 'You either like me or you don't.' It's like those were the words he was thinking."

Okay, Hank, you're creeping me out... and making me feel really guilty right now. You and that dog have the same DNA.

Hank always stood when she entered the room, even this morning when she went to check on the coffee. She had barely been gone long enough for Hank's rear to touch the cushion before he bounced onto his feet as she exited the kitchen.

"You ever have a pet, Christine?"

Hank's words broke her trance.

"Never. Parents wouldn't allow it. I never even got the 'It's a big responsibility' speech or the 'I'm not going to be the one stuck feeding and taking care of him' warning. Always a flat and non-negotiable, 'No!'"

"You should get one now. 'Cause with the right one, Christine, you'll get to experience unconditional love."

She placed a hand on his forearm.

"I bet Henry can say the same thing about you."

The warmth she felt from Hank's arm shocked her, and she stood, flummoxed. "That darned cat. I don't even know who it belongs to. I've never seen it before."

Hank was just as bewildered as Christine. "It's so unlike Henry. He doesn't chase cats. He's usually gentle and kind. I'd swear he wasn't chasing the cat but trying to—"

"Mr. Matthews. I'm Dr. Olson."

Christine, already standing, reached the doctor first. "How's Henry?"

"Mrs. Matthews?"

"Oh, no. I'm... I'm..."

Hank, now standing behind her, answered for her.

"No, this is Miss Kibbe. Christine's a colleague of mine. She drove us here." But there was urgency still in his voice. "Is Henry okay?"

Dr. Olson smiled. "I hate using the expression 'lucky dog,' but that's Henry. We took the x-ray and saw that nothing was fractured, just a dislocation at the hip."

"Thank God."

"Indeed." Christine agreed.

"We did the closed reduction to place the bones back into their proper position. No invasive surgery was needed, but I'll take another x-ray in the morning. Henry is sedated, and he's resting comfortably right now," Dr. Olson explained. "You can see him in a few minutes. I want to keep him overnight. We'll put him in a sling tonight, then we'll get him into a splint of some kind, and hopefully he'll be ready to go home tomorrow."

"Thank you, Doctor." Hank extended his hand.

Dr. Olson shook it. "If you both would like to follow me, I'll take you to see Henry."

Christine stayed rooted in her spot, but as Hank reached the doorway, he turned and motioned her to follow.

"Come on back. I'm sure Henry would love to see you, too."

She tried to fake a smile to match Hank's genuine one.

"Not this time. You should see him alone first."

Hank walked back to her, and for a second she thought he might grab her hand. The touch upon his forearm was distressing enough, she would not react well if he actually led her down the hallway by the hand. The only way to guarantee that would not happen was to follow him willingly.

"If you're sure," she said, causing Hank to smile.

Christine kept her distance while walking down the hallway. In the large room where Henry and other animals were being kept and taken care of, she maintained enough distance to be able to observe Hank without seeming like the social outcast she was starting to realize she really was.

When Hank spotted Henry, Christine was sure she'd seen a small light appear in Hank's eyes. It confirmed to her that Henry and Hank shared something special. And for a moment she felt melancholy. She doubted she ever had that look in her eyes for anyone or was the cause of it in anyone else's.

The man she had all but despised for almost three months hadn't done anything other than be himself. She had been the problem, *the maneater*.

She now realized Hank had put up with her every harsh criticism, tirade, and mood without a single complaint. He had often given in to what she wanted, but he'd also held firm in what he genuinely believed in and felt was right for their assignment. He never harangued or pouted. He was always kind and courteous, and though they were the same age, Hank had never seemed that interested in her as anything other than a coworker.

He was more interested in his dog than her. Worse, he'd rather have the dog as his friend than her.

That says a whole lot about you, Christine, and none of it is good.

She slipped silently back into the hallway and returned to the waiting room. Ensconced in her original spot on the sofa, Christine sat for several minutes, wallowing in self-pity.

Her mind had been so entangled with thoughts that Christine hadn't seen Hank approach.

"I thought you might have left me?"

"Huh?" She shook her head, clearing her cluttered mind but was still able to comprehend his words. "Oh, no. I couldn't—wouldn't."

Hank buried his hands in his pockets.

"Is Henry really all right?" she asked.

"Oh, yeah," Hank assured her. "He's fine. He opened his eyes right after you left."

"Oh, you noticed me leaving." A statement not a question. Her voice betrayed her shame.

"I'm a writer. Like you, I don't tend to miss much."

Oh, Hank, I'm nothing like you... as a writer, and definitely not as a human.

"Not much we can do here," Hank said. "You want to head back and finish the article so I can get out of your hair?"

No, he did not miss much at all, but God only knew how much she had missed.

"No, no. Focus on Henry and forget the assignment for a while. We're actually way ahead of schedule thanks to my OCD tendencies."

"I wouldn't call them tendencies." Hank smiled. "Requirements? Directives? No, mandates."

No man dates! That's how Christine heard the words, and it hit a bit too close to home. *No, I haven't had an actual date in years.*

"Let me take you to dinner since it's obviously too late now for lunch," Hank said.

Her mind was a mess again. Nothing was making sense. His invitation completely shocked her system, but the biggest jolt was her answer.

"I think I'd like that."

Sitting in the passenger seat, Hank buckled his seat belt and looked over at Christine as she was buckling hers. "I guess we won't be eating pizza, huh?"

"Oh? Why not?" As the words crossed over her lips, she was horror-struck and covered her mouth with her right hand. Henry had been hit by the car delivering the pizza they had ordered for lunch.

Hank laughed uproariously, and she noticed the crinkles in the corner of his eyes. She liked his eyes when he laughed. She hadn't noticed that before.

She started her car and drove through the parking lot. Something else drove her thoughts. *Probably because he usually has nothing to laugh about when you're around, Christine.*

"How can you laugh knowing that's what caused Henry's injury?"

"Because Henry would laugh, too," Hank claimed. "Pizza is Henry's favorite food. If he could choose a way to die, death by pizza delivery might be at the top of his list."

"Stop! It's hard enough to merge into traffic without your morbid thoughts."

"I could write an article about him titled 'Death of the Puppy-roni.' Whatcha think?"

"Stop!" Christine tried to speak sternly, but she had to bite her tongue to keep from laughing. "I really can't believe you feed pizza to your dog. Isn't that like a major pet parent faux pas?"

"We avoid the onions, and the place we order from is pretty health conscious and accommodating. They offer gluten free dough. They have a non-garlic version of their sauce as well.

He's a French Bulldog, but that wide body is at least a quarter deep-dish Italian pizza."

Christine smiled. "Guess that makes him a Mutt-zorella."

She watched the crinkles reappear in Hank's eyes, and the inside of the car suddenly seemed a little warmer.

Dining in a low-lighted eatery and being confined within four walls didn't entice either of them. When they drove past a food truck selling tacos of all sorts, and located across from a park, their choices of food and location were set.

They sat on one of the park benches and watched ducks going in and out of the small pond. Christine thought she and Hank would just make small talk, killing time until she drove him home. Instead, Hank was slaying every preconception she had of him.

Her mind became a whirlwind of activity. The events of the day had been completely unexpected. No one would ever hope for Henry or anyone to be injured, but her world was being turned upside down, and she was replaying the afternoon's events to see if she could pinpoint how or why.

She knew, of course, that it all centered around Hank.

Around him, she'd normally have to fight from losing control. In line at the food truck earlier, she'd given up control and allowed him to order for both of them. He ordered fish tacos for himself, adding onions and jalapeños. For her, he ordered steak tacos.

How could he have known her so well? She had to ask.

"You're a Virgo," he said, removing the tacos from the white paper bag. "Virgo's are logical, reliable, and precise."

"And somehow that tells you steak tacos?"

"Somewhat, yes, but—" He paused to sip from the straw in his drink. "But the clincher to your carnivorous habits was you lip syncing that song this morning. *Maneater.*"

Keeping her head down as she unwrapped her first taco, she turned several shades of red. She was mortified and half-hoped she'd hate this taco or at least choke on it. Naturally, it was so delicious that she couldn't wait to tear into the second one.

She'd finished both of hers just as Hank finished his first.

He asked, "Good, I take it?"

"Pretty obvious," she replied, wiping her hands with a napkin. "How's yours?"

Hank tore his last fish taco in two and handed her half. She tried to resist but was inwardly pleased when he insisted.

It was equally scrumptious as her steak tacos had been, and guilt returned after she swallowed the last bite. Though he had readily offered the half, she knew Hank had been starving just as much as she had been. He'd said as much right before he ordered.

The words he'd spoken right after that declaration, to the person taking their order, suddenly came back to Christine.

"For my very good friend here, can I get two of the steak tacos with cilantro, onions, and cheese?"

An unfamiliar heat warmed her blood.

How could you be so wrong about him, Christine? But she already knew the answer to her own question. *Because you were angry with him from the beginning. You never gave him a chance. You were thinking that Hank was somehow taking something from you. You couldn't have been more wrong.*

"And he called me his friend," Christine whispered to herself. "His very good friend."

She had no idea how he could ever say that about her.

Hank stood and took her tray with the used napkins and wrappers. He walked away from her, whistling a familiar song. Eighties-music freak that she was, Simply Red's version of "If You Don't Know Me By Now" was unmistakable.

I SMELLED SOMETHING wonderful the minute I rounded the fence. Since that crazy day over a month ago, I'd avoided coming back here, but I never ventured too far from this neighborhood. Today, without explanation, I felt drawn back to this place.

I heard music coming from the backyard. Someone was playing a song about purple rain. I didn't know rain came in different colors, but the song was nice.

The closer I got to the source of music, I heard ridiculous grunts and chomping. It was coming from behind the corner of the house. If my intuition was correct, I would discover the reason for my return.

I kept close to the fence until I had a clear view of the backyard.

I was right. Feet up, lying on the grass, was that big doofus from before. This time, it wasn't a straw in his mouth that I saw. It was a wooden stick, a small branch from the tree by the picnic table I reasoned.

"That is so pathetically cliché." I announced.

He finally noticed me, and his goofy body started to shake. If I didn't know he was such a doofus, it would have been cute. I might have even felt honored or special. But I didn't. Not really... Okay, maybe just a little.

He tried to roll over on all fours. His hip, in some kind of a harness, made the transition a little difficult.

"No need to get up on my account," I said, making my way towards him.

"Where you been? I wondered what happened to you. You okay? You good? How you doin'?"

Well, whatever his physical injuries were, he was mentally the same.

"Yeah, uh, listen Hemingway..."

"My name's Henry." He was clearly worried. "You don't remember?"

What I remembered was being body-checked into the fence and knocked unconscious. When I came to, I saw two people kneeling over Henry and calling his name. Shaken, but aware of my surroundings, I made my way out of the yard, never to return until today.

"Why'd you do it?" I asked the question that was constantly on my mind.

"Do what?"

"Push me out of harm's way. Take the blow when it should have been me."

"That's what friends do."

"Friend? You don't even know me."

"Doesn't matter."

"Sure it does. You could have been killed trying to save my life."

"And it would have been worth it." Henry hobbled three steps forward. "But we both lived. I'd call that a win-some win-some situation."

"Don't you mean a win-win situation?"

He cocked his head sideways.

"Henry…" This was already hard enough to say without him looking at me sideways. "Thank you. I can never repay you."

"Hungry? I can get you something to eat."

And yet he was still thinking of me.

"No. I'm fine Henry." I started looking for my way out. "Good to see you. Glad you're… you'll be all right, right?"

"Yep. But you're hungry, aren't you?"

I never got a chance to answer.

"WHO'S READY FOR HOMEMADE pizza?" shouted Hank as he exited the sliding door and walked onto the covered patio. "No delivery this time for my boy!" He turned to Christine and added, "And risk a repeat of last month."

"I still can't believe you feed your dog pizza."

"I still can't believe you like '80s music." Hank rolled his eyes in the direction of the music speakers installed in the patio's ceiling.

"Give in, Hank," Christine nudged him playfully. "Hear the music? Get on board the Speedwagon and realize that you really can't fight the feeling."

Christine removed the few items atop the patio table, and Hank set the pizza in the cleared space.

"To the completion of a successful collaboration," Christine declared, opening and then raising her can of Diet Coke.

Hank tipped his water bottle. "And to the best writing partner I've ever had."

"And that would be among how many others exactly?" She knew the answer was zero.

With a grin as wide as could be, Hank answered, "Doesn't remove any truth from my statement, Christine."

Embarrassed, she looked away, spotting Henry slowly heading in their direction.

"It's so good to see Henry out and about. I'm glad he came over to help us celebrate."

"He was sitting by the front door an hour before I was ready to leave," Hank commented. "He was quite eager this morning."

"Well, that might be my fault." Christine clasped her hands behind her back and grinned. "Yesterday, before I left your place, I told him that we would be making pizza."

They both watched Henry make his way across the patio, and instead of sitting near Hank, Henry laid down at Christine's feet. Hank eyed the both of them suspiciously.

"Aren't you two chummy all of a sudden?"

"Jealousy rearing its ugly head?" Christine asked, reaching down to scratch Henry's upturned belly.

"Of a belly rub? Uhh, yes."

Out of the corner of her eye, Christine noticed movement near the back corner of the house.

"Hank. Look!" She pointed forward. "Isn't that the same cat who was here that day?"

"How can you tell, Christine? That was weeks ago."

She grinned, echoing his words from that same day. "I'm a writer. Like you, I don't tend to miss much."

"COME ON. COME ON." Henry was his eager self, calling me forward.

"Aren't you a pretty little thing?" the woman said, looking straight at me.

I turned to see if someone was behind me. Nope. Nobody. I figured they were all as looney as Henry.

The gentleman spoke next. "Looks like you may be hungry."

Okay so Henry's dad had half a brain, so sue me.

I watched as he tore at this triangular piece of bread that was topped with all sorts of things. He put it on a paper plate and set it on the ground next to the one for Henry.

Henry was attacking the contents on his plate. I was hesitant.

"Mrhms, sro groobd."

"Don't talk with your mouth full, Henry."

When Henry finally came up for air, he looked at my plate then at me and then the plate again. "Eat."

"What is this again?"

"Pizza"

"Piece of what though?"

"No. Pizza." He said it slowly like I was stupid or something. "It's good, try it."

I sniffed. It did smell delicious.

"I was wrong," Henry said.

"About?"

"She's not a vegan, but she is an excellent cook. The other day she made chili. Whoo-wee! Shouldn't have had as much as I did. Particularly with my hip still healing. Lordy, I drug my butt across—"

"I'm eating here!" I screeched. "Or at least I'm about to."

"Go ahead. Go ahead. Go ahead."

The French can be so annoying.

"I'm not sure about some of this. Is that cheese?" I asked.

"It is indeed. That's the best part."

"Uh, not for me. I'm fairly sure I'm lactose intolerant. I'll stick to the vegetables on here."

"YOU KNOW WHAT YOU NEED, Christine?"

"No, but I'm sure you're about to tell me."

"You need your own pet," Hank declared, gesturing to the cat near them.

"A cat? Seriously? I heard that you never own a cat, it's more like renting one."

Hank chuckled. "But you didn't completely dismiss the idea, so..."

"I wouldn't even know what to name it. I don't even know if it's a boy or a girl cat."

"It's a her."

Christine glanced down at the two. Henry was attacking his pieces like this would be his last meal. The adorable cat, way too skinny, methodically picked and ate one particular topping.

"There you go, Christine. It's obvious what she likes." Hank reached over and took Christine's hand in his. She did not object.

"You're right. I'll name her Olive."

TODAY

I WAS AGITATED WITH this pink bow Mom attached to my collar. I mean what's up with that?

Now Henry... Oh, Henry! I felt for my friend. Sort of. His dad had put a bowtie around his neck. Most ridiculous thing I had ever seen, but then again, every ridiculous thing I'd ever seen in my life somehow involved Henry.

"Morning, Olive."

"Hello, Henry."

"Ready for the big day?"

"Yeah, whatever."

"By the end of the day, Olive, we're going to be sharing the same house."

"Don't get carried away, Henry, all right? Respect my personal space."

"You won't ever be hungry again."

Yeah, there was that.

"And I'll protect you, and we—"

"Oh, brother."

"That too! We'll be brother and sister."

Henry's dad, and yes, soon to be my stepdad, opened the door that led outside. "Come on you two. Time for the Best Man and Maid of Honor to take their places."

The music choice was lacking if you ask me. I'd actually come to enjoy Mom's musical taste. Whatever that instrumental cacophony was, it was not up to Mom's usual standards.

Had it been me, we would have been listening to some classic hit by Journey or possibly something by Billy Idol.

Nevertheless, I do have to admit, Mom looked stunning coming up the aisle in that white dress.

Once she reached my location, she crouched down and scratched under my chin.

"You look so beautiful, Olive. I'm so glad you've become part of my life."

She even patted Henry's goofy head. "You, too, Mr. Henry."

When she stood next to Hank, I looked at Henry.

"Oh, Henry... Are you crying?"

He showed me his silly grin.

"Isn't it great that we can rescue humans?"

THE END

About the Author

Born and raised in Opelousas, Louisiana, J D Boudreaux is married and has three grown children. The family now resides an hour south in the small town of Erath. A good story, good friends, and a good cup of coffee are the ingredients that make up a great day for J D. Add a little boudin, cracklins, and Momma's homemade carrot cake, and J D will call it a perfect day!

Facebook: https://www.facebook.com/AuthorJDB

Website and Blog: https://sanddollarseries.wixsite.com/authorjdb

Twitter: twitter.com/JD_Boudreaux

Email: authorjdboudreaux@gmail.com

"Grace Shadowed"

A Possession Chronicles short story

By Carrie Dalby

JOHN WOODSLOW WALKED into the back parlor of the Aethelwulf Club, eyes on the graying man amid the dark paneled walls.

Dr. Stephen Moore stood and extended his hand, his bulk towering over the younger man. "Dr. Woodslow, it's a pleasure to meet with you."

"Thank you for arranging the time, Dr. Moore." John firmly shook the offered hand. As soon as they were settled in matching leather wing chairs, a butler poured them each a snifter of brandy. Dr. Moore offered a cigar. John accepted, pleased the older doctor didn't hold back his hospitality before the subject at hand was broached. "Thank you."

When the room cleared of all but a gentleman reading The Daily Register under the corner lamp—newspaper concealing his face—Dr. Moore smiled.

"Well, John, I'm sure you've guessed why I wanted to meet with you. I know word is out that I'm seeking a partner in my practice."

"Yes, Dr. Moore. And I'm honored you thought of me."

"You come highly recommended, having graduated top of your class and doing well in your early years at the hospital, but I have reservations. That's why I wished to meet in an informal setting with you first. I don't want you to get your hopes up too high, young man."

At twenty-six, John was hardly inexperienced, though he knew a doctor over forty would see him as green. "I'm happy to put any of your concerns to rest, Dr. Moore."

"I'm pleased to hear your willingness, but I'm afraid the matters at hand could sully your reputation in the medical field if they prove to be true."

John felt the color drain from his face and glanced nervously at the hidden man in the corner. "I can't think what you might have heard that would sour you toward me."

"Mystics of Dardenne membership for one." Dr. Moore's grin shone more amused than disappointed.

The butler came into the doorway. "Telephone call for you, Dr. Moore."

"I know you understand what life as a doctor is like, but you must excuse me, John. I'll return as soon as possible." Dr. Moore stood and took his hand with the Dardenne handshake.

John stared after the doctor as he left.

Across the room, the newspaper lowered to reveal a smirking Rupert Lyons. "Gave you the old handshake, did he?"

"How did you know?"

Rupert laughed. "You look as though you've seen a ghost and my stint as secretary of the society afforded me the opportunity to peruse the books. I'm happy to report Dr. Moore's years as a member gave a grand showing, even given our record as most debauched. He was head Dardenne in eighty-one when—"

The butler returned to top off the brandy glasses on the side table between the doctors' chairs. Rupert raised his own tumbler and the man saw to it before leaving.

"Then why is he no longer a member if he never married?" John asked.

"Not many Dardennes hold membership for longer than half a dozen years. Those who don't marry tend to step down or are run out well before they turn thirty. We'll get our letters of resignation after this carnival season, with or without a bride to walk down the aisle."

John sucked on the cigar and blew smoke rings as he took a mental tally of the eligible debutantes in the city. Grace Anne Marley always seemed brighter than her peers. Unfortunately, he'd heard too much about her loose ways from other Dardennes to take her seriously.

"Now that my purchase of the Mellings' law firm has been finalized, I'll be staking my claim by New Year's Eve," Rupert warned. "The hurricane in September seems to have all the men in the city on the move. Better choose fast if you want prime pickings. Study the ladies at the Stuarts' Christmas party tomorrow and call dibs before Sean or one of the others step up."

Rupert raised the newspaper as Dr. Moore returned.

"Sorry to keep you waiting, John." He took his former seat and swallowed a shot. "Now, as I was saying, you're at the age of settling down if you wish to remain respectable in society. In order to keep the esteem of my patients, I can only bring in a partner who's in good standing socially. If you'd like to entertain an offer, I insist you revoke your membership and find a respectable wife. There seems to be too many scandals hanging over the Dardennes and debutantes these days, but maybe that's more to do with that gossip magazine than an influx in wanton behavior. That Kate Stuart..." The doctor took another swig. "Whoever chains himself to that firecracker will be in for a treat."

"GRACE ANNE!"

Sadie's shrill voice carried up the stairs to where Grace Anne sat as she fixed her hair at the dressing table. She turned as her sister careened to a stop in the bedroom.

"Grace Anne, you have to help me! It's a matter of life and death!" Anything and everything was a dramatic episode to the twelve-year-old.

She put a hand on Sadie's quaking shoulder. "It can't be all bad."

"But it is! Come to the back porch and see for yourself. Alice and I had to rescue it from her brothers."

Grace Anne groaned. If the Beauchamp boys were involved, there was no telling what mess her sister had gotten herself into. "Judith is picking me up in thirty minutes and I still need to powder my nose."

"You know I wouldn't bother you on a party night if it wasn't important. And we need to move fast before Cook or Nanny notices and tells Mama and Papa when they get home."

She sighed, but followed her sister's blonde pigtails down the front staircase. At times like these, Grace Anne resented being the oldest and having a nine year gap between her and Sadie. Esther, the sister between them, took ill in the yellow fever epidemic nearly a decade prior and didn't survive. Sadie was too young to remember but their parents took years to recover from the loss. Five-year-old Marie wasn't born until 1901, four years after Esther passed away. The three remaining sisters were too spread age wise to be bosom friends and Grace Anne felt more like an aunt than a sister to them.

They exited the house through the dining room and met Alice Beauchamp on the patio. The solemn-faced girl held a rope attached to a mangy brown dog that was knee-high to her. Its matted fur had an odor of the sewer from ten feet away.

"Alice's brothers were tormenting him."

"Of course they were! That beast isn't fit for human companionship." Grace Anne thought of her beloved dog, Flora, who disappeared after she was sent out of town when Esther took ill. She returned to a home devoid of her dear sister and collie.

"It's not his fault he's dirty!" Sadie said with indignation. "Those boys were pulling him through the alleys like he was a tin can on a string. We had to save him, but Alice can't keep him with her brothers around. If you could hide him in your roo—"

"Absolutely not!" Grace Anne crossed her arms over her blue gown. "I don't have time for a filthy mutt, especially with carnival season upon us."

"But if we get him clean, we could give him to Marie for Christmas. Mama wouldn't say no to a present, especially one so cute."

"He's hideous!"

"He's not so bad. And once he's washed and brushed he'll be even sweeter. We've never asked for a dog before, so Mama has never told us no. It'll be the first—"

Grace Anne's chin went up. "I had a gorgeous dog with silky fur. She was the smartest thing this side of Government Street. Esther and I played with her every afternoon and she slept at the foot of my bed each night. There can never be another dog like Flora in this house."

"Please, Grace Anne," Alice said with pleading brown eyes. "I can't hide him from Nanny in my room and if we let him go Richard will kill him."

"That brother of yours is a hooligan, but not a murderer, Alice." Both girls continued to stare at Grace Anne—the dog joining in with sad eyes. "I won't let you bring him inside in his current state."

"We'll wash him out here and brush him real good. We'll work fast before Nanny brings Marie down for supper. I only need to keep him in your room until Mama comes home and it's too late for her to say no. Please, Grace!"

"If he soils anything in my room—"

"He'll be good as gold," Sadie promised with a smile. "Come on, boy."

The two girls led the dog toward the garden spigot, the poor thing limping behind them.

"That dog's lame," Grace Anne called after them.

"He's just tired is all," Alice said. "My brothers wore him out."

The mantel clock chimed through the open door and Grace Anne hurried back to her room to finish preparations for the Stuarts' Christmas party. She wanted to be sure to look appealing enough to catch the eye of one of the handsome bachelors—preferably Dr. Woodslow.

JOHN TRUDGED UP THE front walk of the Victorian monstrosity on Government Street and handed his hat and coat to the help as soon as he was in the door. After the obligatory greeting to Mr. and Mrs. Stuart, he journeyed through the evergreen swags for the sitting room where the younger crowd gathered and forced a smile for the host's daughter.

"It's always good to have a doctor in the house," Kate Stuart simpered as she took in the fit of his black tuxedo. "You are looking especially well tonight, Dr. Woodslow."

"Thank you, Miss Stuart." Unable to find something to compliment her on—other than her well-endowed chest beneath the tight gown—he stopped his greeting at that.

When he tried to continue into the room, she put a hand on his arm. "We seem to have more ladies than gentlemen in attendance tonight. Would you be a dear and spend a little extra time dancing so none of our guests go without?"

"Of course, Miss Stuart."

"It would, after all, be beneficial to you as well. I know Dr. Moore is set on partnering with a family man."

The hurricane might have put an end to Snitch, but magazine or not, Kate was still on top of the gossip game. John nodded to her, hoping she'd release him from her clutches soon. "We're all approaching the settling years."

"Just don't settle for anything short of the best, Dr. Woodslow." She angled toward his ear. "I assure you there are plenty of virginal ladies within these walls tonight. There's no need to be a Davenport with your choice."

"Well said, Miss Stuart." John smirked at the thought of Alexander Melling's ex-fiancée now joined with the most respectable man of their age group in the city. As he helped himself to a glass of eggnog, John wondered if it were possible to find a debutante whom a Mystics of Dardenne member hadn't deflowered. He didn't want to sink himself so low as to court a first year deb, but which lady in the room hadn't felt the groping hands of a Dardenne at a masquerade or entertained more? Probably only Kate Stuart herself as no man would dare attempt anything on that predator.

Thomas and Sean waved him over to the corner. Sipping his drink, he ignored their attempts at conversation as his eyes roamed the sea of colorful gowns across the room. Grace Anne Marley's hour-glass figure filled her royal blue dress perfectly, her golden hair framing her heart-shaped face like a halo. Her nose was a little too sharp, but those lips made up for it. If it weren't for the fact that Sean and several others had boasted about kissing her, he would have declared himself to her when they danced at The Point Clear Hotel the weekend before the hurricane.

Rupert joined them.

"Did you do it?" Sean asked.

"I have her father's permission." Rupert grinned.

Sean slugged Rupert and laughed. "I don't envy you that prize, Lyons."

"What?" John looked between the two.

"Did you not hear anything we were talking about?" Sean gave him a scowl before continuing. "Rupert asked Mr. Stuart's permission to court Kate."

John choked on the eggnog, sputtering until Thomas slapped him on the back—which, thanks to Thomas's boxing hobby, nearly sent him face-first onto the Oriental rug.

Rupert leaned closer once the coughing subsided. "She may be a frigid bitch, but I know where to get what I want. Even though Consuela left town this autumn, there are plenty more to choose from. And what better way is there to avoid being gossiped about than by marrying the source of the chatter? Kate is all about saving face. She'd never speak ill of me to anyone."

Though impressed with Rupert's business plan for marriage, John couldn't get over the idea of marrying a woman he had no desire for. Life was too short for that. He wanted respectability and love. He'd be too busy with work to see to a woman at home and then seek release elsewhere. It was already rare he entered the red light district outside of carnival season. His lack of time and energy was to blame because—unlike his lawyer friends—his job was physically demanding and took more hours from his day.

A few minutes later, a string quartet began playing across the hall. Rupert offered his arm to Kate and they led a procession to the ballroom. As couples paired off, John ditched his tumbler on the credenza and approached Grace Anne.

He bowed before her. "Would you do me the honor of this dance, Miss Marley?"

With a beguiling smile, she dipped into a curtsy that showcased her décolletage. "It would be my pleasure, Dr. Woodslow."

Keeping his hands in respectable locations as they waltzed, John couldn't help but stare at Grace Anne's perfectly bowed pink lips. At least they weren't red from use like they often were at gatherings. Maybe tonight he'd be the one to bring color to those succulent petals.

"Have you had a pleasant December thus far, Miss Marley?"

"Yes, though my hands are full at the moment. My parents are in Birmingham for a week and my younger sisters always manage to court trouble, especially the middle one as she's old enough to go about without Nanny."

John smiled down at her, happy to hear she wasn't overly strained with the care of rambunctious children—for he wanted a few of his own one day. "Nothing too troubling, I hope."

"She brought a mangy dog home," Grace Anne blurted, showcasing her manners weren't as refined as some of the other ladies.

John laughed and enjoyed the way her eyebrows pinched together as she flashed a quick frown.

"It's not only that," she continued. "Sadie expects me to keep the dog hidden in my room until Christmas. She wants to give it to Marie, our youngest sister, so our parents can't turn it out."

"Would they turn out a helpless puppy?"

"It's not a puppy, Dr. Woodslow. It's a dog. A filthy little beast it looked too." Grace Anne's cheeks turned rosy.

"Do you not like dogs?"

"I have nothing against them. I had my own as a girl." Grace Anne shuddered and a shadow crossed her face.

John instinctively held her closer. "What is it, Miss Marley?"

Her eyes widened and she appeared to blink back tears. "Nothing, Dr. Woodslow. But that creature was not fit for proper living in the state it was in."

The song came to an end and he took her by the elbow, not wanting to let her go. "May I escort you to the refreshment table?"

"No, thank you. You've been most kind."

He reluctantly watched her leave. Heading for a tray of wine being brought around the ballroom, John found himself reaching for a glass at the same time as Dr. Moore.

"While it's good to see you dancing with an eligible young lady, please keep in mind that one's father has had his fortune less than a decade and she was unfortunately linked with Lucille Easton as recently as two years ago."

John felt his cheeks go red and smoothed a hand over his slicked back hair in desperate need of a trim. "Miss Marley was on a European tour with her family when the scandal happened. I hardly see how that impugns her character."

"Those young ladies were dearest friends, were they not?"

"I cannot say." John kept his gaze on the doctor's. "I haven't a younger sister or connection to either of them other than through Edmund Easton, who was just as shocked as the rest of us over the fall of his sister."

The knowing look in the older doctor's eyes was one of amusement as he patted John's back. "Choose wisely, Dr. Woodslow."

GRACE ANNE STOOD WITH a chattering Judith McGowan—her companion for the night—but all she could think about was the feeling of being in John's arms. It had been three months since she'd spoken to him. The previous time was a September night across the bay during the celebration for Alexander Melling and his Yankee fiancée, Beatrice Kirkpatrick. The New Yorker was elegant, but no match for how he and Lucy must have looked together. Having missed her best friend's first relationship and its aftermath, Grace Anne resented her European travels. If she had been home, she could have kept Lucy from losing her head over a smooth talker like Alexander. But she was pleased to know her dearest friend was now settled with a gentleman. Frederick Davenport had always been kind to Grace Anne when she was playing at the Eastons'—even before her father's lumber business took off during the Spanish-American War.

Kate joined the group emanating a surprising glow.

Hoping to keep Kate focused on her own affairs rather than sniffing out news about Grace Anne's dance partner, she focused the conversation on her. "Do you find Mr. Lyons to be a good dancer, Kate?"

"Of course he is." She checked the time on the pocket watch on her necklace, as though down-playing the excitement in her voice.

"He's nowhere near as fine as Alexander Melling was," Judith said. "He was a scoundrel, but the best dancer in town, though Frederick Davenport is light on his feet as well. Is he here tonight?"

Kate snorted back a laugh. "My parents wouldn't invite that trollop he married into our home. Becoming Mrs. Davenport doesn't make a lady out of a fallen woman. Poor F.L.D. will turn into a hermit from lack of invitations this Mardi Gras season."

"Still," Judith said, "Mr. Lyons isn't as good a dancer as Mr. Davenport."

"He's a thousand times more functional on the dance floor—and other places I bet—than the ancient man you keep making eyes at. And he asked me to call him Rupert." Kate turned away from Judith with a sneer.

"Mr. Smith is a seasoned businessman," Judith retorted. "What's a twenty-year difference anyway? If he doesn't last long, at least his money will. Rupert Lyons is nothing but an upstart lawyer with well-connected relatives."

Kate turned back, her watch lifting from her chest with the quick motion. "Haven't you heard, Judith? Rupert bought the newly renamed Lyons, Melling, and Associates. He now owns one of the longest established law firms in the city."

Judith's torso hardly moved within her tightly strung corset, but Grace Anne could tell she huffed for breath. "But he's still a crooked nose cad like the rest of his friends."

Rolling her eyes, Kate went for the hall.

"Have you danced with Rupert Lyons?" Judith asked Grace Anne.

"Unfortunately."

"See! He's nothing to get worked up over, especially compared to a man like Frederick Davenport. Kate can say what she wants about Lucille Easton, but that girl has to have something we don't to land a man like that with her reputation."

Grace Anne held her tongue, refusing to speak of her former best friend though she knew Frederick had loved Lucy since childhood. He was the type of man to remain loyal, no matter what.

"But that Dr. Woodslow," Judith continued. "He's nearly as fine to look at and seems smitten with you tonight, Grace Anne."

"Do you think so?" She cursed the eager tone in her voice when Judith responded with a toothy smile. "I mean, he is handsome, but I—"

"He's coming this way."

Grace Anne felt the blood leave her face and forgot how to breathe as John came to a stop beside her.

"Are you all right, Miss Marley?"

Managing to nod, she gazed up at John, focusing on his strong jaw as she wondered what it would feel like to kiss him.

"She does look pale, doesn't she?" Judith took a step away. "Why don't you take her to get some air, Dr. Woodslow? The veranda can be reached through the dining room."

Judith winked at Grace Anne as John led her toward the hall. The brisk night air kept the party indoors, but Grace Anne was no stranger to dark locations. She'd often gone off with dance partners to show them the kissing skills she'd perfected from her time toying with chauffeurs and the brothers of her friends.

John stopped beside a trailing bougainvillea, the white railing and columns behind him a striking contrast to his black tuxedo and the dark vine. His touch lowered from her elbow, caressing her white gloves until he held her hand. "Are you well, Miss Marley?"

If it wasn't so chilly, she would have melted at the sound of the concern in his voice. "I'm only worried about that stupid dog and what mess might await me at home."

His grin was charming even in the dim space. "I'm afraid I can't help you much with that."

Still holding her hand, she half wished he'd steal a kiss like his friends always did—but the other half was glad he didn't if it meant he respected her. Or maybe he had no interest, though Judith was seldom wrong when it came to what men wanted. Testing her sway over him, Grace Anne tilted her head and pursed her lips ever so slightly.

John squeezed her hand. "Has anyone told you that you're a beguiling figure, Miss Marley?"

"No, Dr. Woodslow," she whispered.

"But surely they must have, with all the men—"

Grace Anne yanked her hand free and stepped back. "Just what do you mean by that?"

"I didn't—"

"Surely you don't think me dim-witted enough to believe there's no accusation when a man refers to all the men in regards to a lady? Just what do you think all these men are doing?"

"Kissing you, Miss Marley," he said with shame. "What man could resist your perfect lips?"

"Surely you can, Dr. Woodslow. We've been acquainted several years now and you've yet to do more than dance a few times with me. Are you morally stronger than all the other suitors you accuse me of being fresh with or am I beneath your appeal?" Her hands were on her hips now.

Cheeks ruddy, John met her glare with a soft gaze. "Neither of those things. Please forgive my poor word choices."

She shook her head, not wishing to think about John knowing all of her exploits—however innocent they seemed at the time. "Please excuse me, Dr. Woodslow."

THE NEXT MORNING, JOHN stood between Rupert and Sean on the cathedral portico. The three bowed to the widow in black when Mrs. Melling walked by, but soon returned to their whispered conversation.

"And you didn't even kiss her?" Sean looked incredulous.

John shook his head.

"There's definitely something wrong with your approach if you didn't get any action from Grace Anne," Rupert smirked. "The only deb more willing than her is Judith, though she's mellowed a bit now that she's working the older crowd. Mark my words—Judith will be on the arm of a rich widower before Fat Tuesday."

Sean laughed. "And she'll be back on the market within a decade. As long as she keeps those measurements, she'll have no problem scoring another pay day."

"Excuse me, gentlemen." Rupert straightened his tie and descended the steps, offering his arm to Kate when she entered the churchyard with her family.

John cleared his throat and looked at his friend. "How far have you gone with Miss Marley?"

"It's been two years, but it's not something to forget." Sean laughed and slapped John on the back. "Relax, Woodslow. She's not like my Eliza. She's more than willing to kiss, but she's no pushover. I know for a fact she's slapped Thomas and a few others who went for a feel though they'll deny it and claim they won the prize."

He smiled as the woman herself entered the gate. The three Marley sisters with their varying shades of blonde hair were a bright spot amid the Sunday crowd. Grace Anne held the hand of the youngest tucked into her own and the middle sister—the one causing her trouble—followed behind them. On the portico, they paused as Grace Anne removed their mantillas from her reticule. Watching the motherly sight of her pinning the head coverings on the girls spurred John to action.

Reaching the door nearest them, John held it open for Grace Anne with a bow. "Good morning, Miss Marley."

"Good morning, Dr. Woodslow." She gave a shallow nod and went through the door without a smile, though the middle sister turned to stare at him.

Sean came to his side. "What did happen between the two of you last night?"

"I fear I made a muddle of things when I alluded to all the men she might—"

Sean laughed. "I knew you weren't as smooth as Easton, but of all the things to say to a woman, that's the worst!"

"Think she'll ever forgive me?"

With a hand clapped on his shoulder, Sean led him into the cathedral. "What girl could resist a Dardenne? Give her time."

But did he have time with Dr. Moore seeking to fill the role of a partner? And would Grace Anne be acceptable in the older doctor's eyes?

AFTER SUNDAY SUPPER, Grace Anne came to terms with what she hoped to avoid. Staring at the chocolate brown dog that followed her around whenever she was in her room, she could no longer pretend its limp wasn't increasing. A whine even accompanied it every few steps. Seeking to provide a bit of relief for the creature, she sat at her desk. The dog immediately settled at Grace Anne's feet. Reluctantly, she reached down and rubbed behind its ears. Her hand then trailed down to the dog's back, fingers threading through the long fur that was softer than she expected.

After hearing Nanny bring Marie down the hall from the bathroom to the nursery, Grace Anne slipped out of her room to the telephone in her father's study on the main floor. She waited while the operator looked up the number and connected her to the other extension.

"Dr. Woodslow's residence," the voice of a housekeeper or cook came across the line.

"Is the doctor available?" Grace Anne asked.

"Yes, ma'am. May I ask who's calling?"

"Grace Anne Marley."

She twisted a finger around the cord of the earpiece as she waited.

"Miss Marley?"

"I'm sorry to bother you, Dr. Woodslow, but there's a medical issue in my house. I was wondering if you would be able to examine the patient."

"I'd be delighted to, Miss Marley. Is half an hour soon enough?"

"That would be perfect. Thank you. I'll leave the front door unlocked. You may let yourself in so my sisters aren't unnecessarily disturbed. I'll wait for you in the parlor, just to the left upon entering."

"I'll be there as quick as possible, Miss Marley."

Grace Anne said goodnight to Marie and made sure Sadie was settled in her room with a book before collecting the dog. She bundled it in a blanket to carry the poor thing downstairs so no fur would mar the front of her red Sunday dress. After putting the blanket in the corner, she sat in one of the armchairs. Grace Anne was pleased her coldness to the doctor at the cathedral that morning didn't affect his willingness to help.

Five minutes later, John silently stepped into the parlor carrying a black bag.

"The door, please, Dr. Woodslow." When he closed it, she stood. "Thank you for coming so promptly."

He grinned and smoothed a hand over his dark-blond hair that showcased a schedule too busy to visit the barber as often as his friends. "I'm happy to be of service, Miss Marley. I do hope you'll forgive my fumbling words."

Her cheeks heated at him bringing up the unladylike behaviors he alluded to the night before. "Let us speak no more of it, Dr. Woodslow. Are you ready to see the patient?"

"Of course. Which sister is ill? They both looked to be in the peak of health at Mass this morning." He turned for the door. "Or is it one of the help?"

Grace Anne crossed the room to him, the dog jumping from its blanket to follow. "Here, Dr. Woodslow. See how he limps?"

John watched the dog for a few seconds before staring at Grace Anne in disbelief.

"Sadie thought he was simply tired from being strung about by the Beauchamp boys, but it's only gotten worse." She pointed to the floor. "The dog, Dr. Woodslow, or have I grown a second nose that I'm not aware of?"

"I am no veterinarian, Miss Marley. I have been schooled and trained to work exclusively with humans, not animals." His handsome face set in a grimace of indignation.

"Then I suppose I should have called Dr. Hughes. I remember he always gave Flora a checkup when he came to examine me or Esther."

John's face softened before a chuckle escaped. "I'll have to remember that if I move from the hospital to doing regular house calls. Kindness to an animal would be the best way to the heart of an uncooperative child."

It was Grace Anne's turn to take a defiant stance. "First a wanton and now an uncooperative child. Never in all my life have I been subject to such uncouth accusations!"

"You misunderstand me once again." He set his bag on the nearest chair and moved toward her.

She crossed her arms and sidestepped. "Don't try to take it back. I know perfectly well when I'm being insulted."

"I'd never wish to insult or harm you, Miss Marley." His hand settled on her shoulder. "I'm forever saying the wrong things because you make me feel like a schoolboy before your beauty. My brain runs through a heap of jealous thoughts and my heart beats quicker than my mouth can run. Forgive me for falling under your spell."

A smile of relief found her lips. "You don't think ill of me?"

"Never, Miss Marley."

With a flood of relief, Grace Anne's arms were about his neck, hands playing in the hair that grew over his stiff collar as she angled for his mouth. Pleased John could be bold, she reveled in his taste as his arms encircled her waist. She pressed against him and enjoyed the surge of delight their bodies together brought her.

As though taking her motion as an invitation for more, John's hands roamed her back until they settled on her hips with a kneading motion that made Grace Anne's body tingle with passion. The kisses turned ardent and he worked his lips to the red ruffle at her throat.

She gasped. "Dr. Woods—"

"Call me John, Gracie." He kissed his way back to her lips, planting one there before pulling back enough to look her in the eyes as he ran a thumb across her cheek.

MAYBE HE DID WRONG by calling her by a pet name before Grace Anne even asked for him to call her by her given one, but it fell from his lips as natural as azaleas blooming in March.

"John," her red lips curved prettily as she whispered, "I don't know what you've heard, but please know I've never allowed a man to hold me like this."

He shushed her with a finger on her mouth—which urged him to lean in for another taste of her sweetness. "As long as I'm the only one you give your kisses to from now on."

Her hug was tight and the feeling of her bosom pressed against him was nearly too much. "I've had my eyes on you a long time, John Woodslow. Every time I practiced kissing, I imagined it was you. I hope I didn't disappoint."

"Let's not start in on that again." He laughed and stroked her arm in an attempt to erase all the stories he'd heard about her. "But you're wonderful, Gracie. And I've been watching you as well."

At their feet, the dog shifted and whined.

"Oh, the poor dear!" Grace Anne bent to retrieve the dog.

"It appears you've taken a liking to him since you cared enough to phone a doctor. Or was that a ruse to get me here for a kiss?" He winked as she blushed.

"He's really much better looking since Sadie and Alice cleaned him up. I believe he has a bit of terrier in him. Of course he doesn't compare to my old girl. Flora was twice this size and her coat was long and silky."

"Set him down a moment so I can see how he stands." John stood back and noticed the way the dog favored its front right paw. He motioned to the blanket. "Is it all right to use this to examine him on?"

Grace Anne quickly spread it over the settee and knelt on the floor beside the dog she'd placed on the blanket.

John got his bag and joined Grace Anne, retrieving the necessary supplies from the case before angling the side table lamp to shine on his four legged patient. Slipping the metal band for his head mirror over his hair, he adjusted the disc so he could see perfectly through the center hole with his left eye. He chanced a look at Grace Anne—the brightness of the reflected light making her creamy complexion glow. He wished the dog wasn't in pain, for he wanted nothing more than to hold her once more, but he silently blessed the mutt for bringing them together.

"Hold him steady, Gracie."

She leaned over the dog with one arm, its affected paw tight in her other grip. John angled closer and the gleam of the mirror immediately caught something in its light. Carefully spreading the fur between the pads of the paw, he licked his lips and held his breath before gingerly touching the object. The dog whined and tried to wince, but Grace Anne held him firm.

"What is it?" she whispered.

"Looks like a piece of glass." He took the scissors in hand. "Let me trim some of these hairs and get a better look."

Trimming done, John turned to Grace Anne. "Would you like to see it through my head mirror?"

"No." She shuddered and buried her face in the dog's coat. "Please hurry and get it out."

"I assume you had no romantic notions of nursing if you can't even bear a bit of glass in a dog."

"No, never. I tend to faint at the sight of blood."

"And yet you've set your sights on a doctor," John teased.

"I might change my mind," she said as she took a coquettish glance at him.

He filched a kiss from her before she could protest. "Don't you dare, Gracie. You're even more amusing than I imagined."

"I shall add amusing to the ever growing list of insults you're unintentionally labeling me with."

"Will I forever be sticking my foot in my mouth around you?"

"I hope so, for it would mean I'll see you again."

John returned her smile before focusing on the task of removing the inch long piece of glass with a steady hand.

"I need alcohol," he said upon removal as he held a clean cloth to the paw. "I've got him."

Grace Anne hurried across the room to a decanter set and returned with two glasses. "Do you always celebrate after a successful operation?"

John laughed so hard he dropped his hold on the cloth. Grace Anne set the drinks on the coffee table and paled at the sight of the bloody linen. Turning to her, John took the nearest tumbler and brought it to her lips. "Drink it quick, my dear. It'll set you to rights."

She downed the whiskey and coughed. John continued to chuckle as he held her upright with a loving arm.

"How old are you, Gracie?"

"Twenty-one last September." Her cheeks were now rosy with health.

"Forgive me for adding another vulgarity to my ever growing list, but how did you manage to make it to twenty-one when you're delightfully naïve about so many things?"

Rather than watch the spark of anger in her eyes, John turned his attention back to the dog. After pouring the contents of his glass over the wound and applying pressure for another minute, he wrapped the paw with fresh bandages from his bag.

"There." He sat back on his heels. "I can honestly say that's the finest paw I've ever tended. Now, do you think I could get a drink I'll be able to enjoy this time?"

AFTER HIS MONDAY MORNING rounds in the hospital, a visitor waited for John in the doctor's lounge.

Dr. Moore snuffed his cigarette in the nearest ashtray. "Did I not make myself clear, Dr. Woodslow?"

"Sir?" John closed the door behind him and prayed no one would enter until the conversation was over.

"About that Marley girl not being the right sort of doctor's wife for my partner. I was leaving a house call at the Powells' across the street after ten o'clock last night and saw her accompany you out onto her porch. I know her parents are out of town and—"

Indignation over the reproachful tone regarding the woman he loved surged through John. "I may be on staff at the hospital, Dr. Moore, but I have been known to take house calls when the need arises. I'll have you know Miss Grace Anne Marley assisted me in a medical procedure for someone in her household. She bravely sat with the patient to offer comfort while I removed a glass splinter from a limb. Then she helped with the sanitation of the wound afterward. If that doesn't sound like a doctor's wife, I don't know what actions would."

"Well..." Dr. Moore puffed his cheeks with a flustered exhalation. "There's still the issue of her friendship with Lucille Easton."

"Perhaps you don't know because you weren't the physician who attended the families, but Miss Marley lost a sister during the yellow fever epidemic of ninety-seven along with the Eastons' three children, all close in age to Lucille. The two bonded in their grief, Dr. Moore, because they both had heartaches not many other children could relate to." John was pleased to have learned that information himself the previous night during a quiet chat over coffee while the dog convalesced on the sofa. "They shared books and daydreams like well-bred girls do in their tender years. They never went about wantonly on the town or any such nonsense you seem determined to believe of

Miss Marley because of her childhood friendship with another girl in mourning."

Dr. Moore smoothed his suit jacket as he stood. "It seems you've taken this all to heart, Dr. Woodslow. I'm happy to see you're thinking things through, but do remember the citizens of Mobile don't always know the intricacies of a person's personal life. They only know what they've seen and heard. When they choose a doctor they want respectability."

"As you've said yourself," John said with a smile, "I'm doing well at the hospital. Patients who find themselves within these walls are often too far gone to care what the gossip was about a physician or his wife from years back. They only care that the hands are capable. And the board of directors will see the statistics of those cared for and medical achievements when selecting a head surgeon."

The older doctor laughed. "You're intelligent to the end, Dr. Woodslow. I wish you the best."

"Thank you, Dr. Moore." He offered his hand.

"And she's a vivacious young lady. Just the type to satisfy a Mystics of Dardenne member."

"Was there no one sprightly enough in your day, Dr. Moore?"

"Only one," Dr. Moore said with a smile. "Another Dardenne may have taken Ruth down the aisle, but I got to her first."

GRACE ANNE ENTERED the parlor Monday night, her shadow directly behind the train of her tea gown. While she carried the dog up and down the stairs when it needed to go out, Shadow made fine progress for short trips around her room that day. Settled into the corner of the settee, the shaggy dog curled on the rug beside her.

John let himself in a few minutes later. His grin lit the room and Grace Anne found herself rising to meet him. The dog came directly behind her and John dropped to a knee to look him over.

"If I'm going to come in second to patients, Dr. Woodslow, I'll have to rethink allowing you to court me."

"Well Miss Marley," he said with his drawling charm as he looked up at her, "I'd say seeing our patient is doing well is a cause for celebration. We make a good team, you and I. Another dose of alcohol is just what the doctor orders if all is well, but first I need to inspect the wound."

She motioned to the folded towel on the settee with an air of superiority.

Standing, he took her by the waist and kissed her hard. "And today someone had the nerve to tell me you wouldn't make a proper doctor's wife."

"Yet another insult!" She tried to squirm away, but he held fast.

His warm lips were at her neck, breath in her ear before he whispered. "You may be certain, Gracie dear, that I praised your bravery and comforting abilities when you worked diligently beside me. I hope you'll do as well tonight and we're able to enjoy another conversation afterward."

Feeling completely adored within his arms, Grace Anne pressed her mouth to his and threaded her fingers through his unruly hair.

"Is my sister paying for house calls with affections?" Sadie asked from the doorway.

Grace Anne turned to the door. "Of all the—"

"Come now, Miss Sadie. You know better," John said as he approached the girl in her nightdress. "Your sister and I have a connection deeper than the dog. I respect her too much to accept payment for tending to someone within these walls—human or otherwise."

"Grace Anne said Shadow's better. Is he truly?"

"Shadow is it?" He smiled and looked from Grace Anne to the dog at her feet. "So they've both taken a liking to each other enough to earn a fitting name. The only way to know for sure is to check the wound. Miss Sadie, would you care to be my assistant when I remove the bandage?"

"Yes, please!" Sadie took the doctor's hand.

"But only if you promise to go straight back to bed as soon as Shadow's tended," Grace Anne added.

"Yes, yes. Anything!"

John motioned them toward the settee and set about arranging his supplies. He pulled a bottle of clear alcohol from his bag. "So I'm not accused of using up your daddy's good whiskey on a dog."

Grace Anne placed Shadow in her lap and allowed Sadie to hold the affected paw over the towel so her sister had full view of the happenings instead of her.

"No sign of infection and the swelling is significantly less than it was yesterday," John declared. "It appears your big sister is a better nurse than she expected."

Sadie giggled and then John poured the alcohol over the wound. The dog whined but held still until the paw was wrapped once more. Then Shadow licked John's face before jumping down and lying at Grace Anne's feet.

"Go on to bed now, Sadie," Grace Anne said gently.

The girl stopped beside John as he repacked his medical bag. "Will you have to see Shadow again? Our parents come home tomorrow and he's supposed to be a secret."

"I most certainly will make inquiries over my patient. I've grown rather fond of Shadow and wish to speak to your father about bringing him to my house in the future."

"But I wanted to give him to Marie for Christmas!"

"That dog has chosen your big sister, Sadie. Don't give Shadow to anyone else because I aim to take care of them both."

Sadie caught on with a blush and giggled. "Yes, Dr. Woodslow. Goodnight, and thank you for helping Shadow."

Once they were alone, Grace Anne extended her hand to him. "Do you really mean it, John?"

He pressed his lips to each knuckle. "With all my heart, Miss Marley. I'll declare my intentions to your father tomorrow evening and ask permission to escort you to Christmas Mass and Order of Mayhem's New Year's Eve ball so all of Mobile will know the best kisser in the city is off the market."

"Will you ever learn to pay me a compliment without shaming?"

"I'll keep trying, Gracie, if you can keep on forgiving me."

"I'll do my best, but you better pray Shadow's sore foot is the only wound you'll need to heal between us." She tugged him to the settee beside her. Their kiss broke when Shadow jumped into Grace Anne's lap. She rubbed the dog's ears and looked to John with a playful smile. "You may keep company with some scoundrel friends, but Shadow will protect me. He'll not stand by and allow my heart to be broken."

His arms were about her waist, a smolder in his eyes that promised a lifetime of passion. "You could do no better in life than with a faithful dog and loving husband. And you'll always possess my heart with your enticing ways. Though please remember, I am good with stitching if the need arises."

THE END

About the Author

While experiencing the typical adventures of growing up, Carrie Dalby called several places in California home, but she's lived on the Alabama Gulf Coast since 1996. Serving two terms as president of Mobile Writers' Guild and five years as the Mobile area Local Liaison for the Society of Children's Book Writers and Illustrators are two of the writing-related volunteer positions she's held. When Carrie isn't reading, writing, browsing bookstores/libraries, or homeschooling her children, she can often be found knitting or attending concerts.

Besides *The Possession Chronicles*, Carrie has published two young adult novels—*Fortitude* (listed as a Best Historical Book for Kids by Grateful American Foundation) and *Corroded*—as well as several short stories in different anthologies.

For more information, visit Carrie Dalby's website: https://carriedalby.com/

Join her monthly newsletter for behind the scene tidbits: https://mailchi.mp/0aa35165c959/httpscarriedalby-comnewsletter

Find Carrie on:

Goodreads: https://www.goodreads.com/author/show/14682659.Carrie_Dalby

Facebook: https://www.facebook.com/CarrieDalbyAuthor/

Twitter: https://twitter.com/wonderwegian

Instagram: https://www.instagram.com/carriedalbyauthor/

BookBub: https://www.bookbub.com/profile/carrie-dalby

And on Pinterest, where you can find lots of visuals for *The Possession Chronicles* and other goodies: https://www.pinterest.com/wonderwegian/

"Smokey Finds a Home"

By Sharon Marchisello

The kittens were almost eight weeks old now, and it was time to cull. The good ones—the perfect Siamese specimens—would be sold to pet stores. The others went away.

The more kittens the owner of the pet store accepted the better the family's Christmas would be.

Ashley shivered as she stroked the babies, tickling their fat little bellies and rubbing their chins, their tiny paws wrapping around her fingers. Their litter box needed changing, but her nose had become numb to the odor. She would get to it later today.

She picked up each kitten, inhaling its milky smell. She cuddled it against her peach-soft cheek and then kissed its tiny furry head before setting it gently back into the wire cage to play with its littermates. When the kittens were tired of playing, they gathered into piles to sleep, warming themselves and drawing comfort from each other's bodies.

She always hated this time. She loved all the kittens, and wanted to keep them all. But Mama and Daddy would not let her. She was only allowed to play with the kittens if she promised not to fuss when it was time to cull.

"Silly girl, you don't want to grow up to be a crazy cat lady. Think of how bad the house would smell," Daddy teased. Already, the litter box was becoming unmanageable, and the four kittens strained and cried to get out of their cage so they could explore their surroundings. They were getting bigger and stronger, and they resisted her efforts to stuff them back inside the cage when she was finished petting them more forcefully than ever before.

Choco, Simba, and Tonya were perfect specimens, and to-morrow, Ashley predicted, they would go to the pet store. Soon someone would buy them and take them home and maybe love them as much as she did. Someone would get to watch them grow into beautiful cats, play with them, make them part of their family.

But Smokey was flawed. Daddy had already said so. Smokey had white paws, and they weren't even symmetrical. A hint of tabby stripes peeked through his lilac point tail. And there was something wrong with one of his clear blue eyes, an infection that wouldn't go away. Daddy had tried several medications, but nothing worked, so he gave up. He didn't like wasting money on the kittens—especially the ones the pet store man wouldn't take. Margins were thin and veterinary care cut into the profits.

Ashley held Smokey tightly and listened to him purr. He was the sweetest kitten in Samantha's fifth litter; if only Daddy would let her keep him. She didn't see what the harm would be. He wouldn't sell, so keeping him wouldn't eat into the profits.

She longed to have a kitten of her own, watch it grow up, have it become her pet, and her best friend. Kittens listened when she told them her problems. How the kids made fun of her at school because of the limp she'd had all her life. She'd never thought much about it until they called her names like "Gimpy" and "Crip." It was so hard to make friends, to join into the conversation without being ridiculed or called "Stupid." The kittens never judged her, never interrupted, never told her she didn't try hard enough, like Mama and Daddy often did. The kittens just purred and cheered her up when she was sad. Oh, how she wanted a kitten...

But Mama was allergic to cats. No animals in the house, that was the rule.

And these cats were not pets. Daddy and Mama constantly had to remind her of that fact. Purebred Siamese cats were a business, a major source of income for the family; they helped them make ends meet. The kittens' home was the detached garage. It was cold in the winter and hot in the summer, even with fans running, but it didn't matter, because it was only a temporary home until they could go to their real homes, their forever homes.

Reluctantly, Ashley shut off the space heater that had taken some of the chill out of the room. She couldn't leave it on unattended; there was too much danger of the heater sparking a fire. Better that the kittens feel cold than to burn up in a fire, Daddy always said. She headed back inside knowing Mama and Daddy would be out soon looking for her, and Daddy would be angry if he found her in the garage with the kittens again.

She slipped into the house through the back door and remembered not to slam it. The party was still going on, so no one noticed her. Gripping the banister, she limped upstairs to her tiny bedroom where she was supposed to be doing her homework.

Christmas music played through the television in the living room. Cheerful voices grew louder as the night wore on and the alcohol flowed. The raucous singing started.

Everyone seemed happy, anxiously looking forward to the holidays. So why was she so sad?

THE NEXT MORNING, ASHLEY got up early and, still in her pajamas, rushed out to the garage to say good-bye to the kittens. She picked up each one, kissed its tiny head, and then placed it back in the cage. Smokey seemed especially clingy today.

Car tires crunched the gravel driveway, and then the motor shut off. A metallic door slammed. Ashley could hear Daddy talking to the owner of the pet store.

She had an idea. She opened a deep file drawer in Daddy's big wooden desk and let Smokey crawl inside. "Shhh..." she whispered, placing a finger over her lips.

Smokey looked up at her with his trusting blue eyes. The flawed one was watering again, but she didn't have time to wipe it. She closed the desk drawer just as the side door to the garage opened. Daddy and the pet store owner entered the room.

The man who owned the pet store reeked of cigarette smoke. He ran his stubby fingers along the cages. He opened the one where Samantha's litter stayed, roughly picked up each kitten to examine it critically, then shoved it back inside. Tonya cried out and almost bit him as he twisted her little body upside down.

Ashley winced. It was all she could do to stop herself from hurling herself at the man to make him stop hurting Tonya.

As expected, the pet store owner chose Choco, Simba, and Tonya from Samantha's litter. As usual, he tried to talk Daddy into lowering his price, but as usual, Daddy wouldn't budge. Grumbling, the man paid Daddy with a dirty wad of cash and stuffed his purchases into hard plastic pet carriers. The cage where Samantha's kittens had lived now stood empty.

Ashley smiled at Daddy after the pet store owner had left with his mewling carriers. "We sold all the kittens," she said proudly. "We're going to have a good Christmas."

Daddy's eyes narrowed. "Where's that runt with the white paws?" Of course, he did not speak of Smokey by name. None of the kittens were supposed to have names, since they didn't stay here long. If Ashley had mentioned Choco, Simba, and Tonya, Daddy would not have known whom she was talking about.

Not looking at her father, Ashley murmured, "I thought the pet store man took the whole litter." She gestured toward the empty cage, ready to be cleaned and prepared for the next litter of kittens.

Just then a squeaky "meow" erupted from the direction of Daddy's desk. "Where did you hide the cat?" Daddy asked Ashley. His dark brown eyes focused on her face like a laser. They followed her eyes to the desk where she'd hidden Smokey.

Ashley hung her head. Daddy had warned her about interfering. What would be her punishment? Would she be allowed to play with the next litter of kittens?

She bent and retrieved Smokey from the file drawer. He was purring, as if he'd thoroughly enjoyed his adventure. "Daddy, can't I keep him?"

Daddy grabbed the kitten from his daughter's small hands. "No, sweetheart. You know better than to ask." He touched her chin with one hand, while clutching Smokey in the other. "Cheer up. Samantha is pregnant again. There'll be another litter of kittens soon."

Ashley nodded. And she would love them all just as much. Her lip trembled. It was still hard to say good-bye. It got harder with each litter. "Daddy, where will you take him?" She knew she was not supposed to ask, but she couldn't help herself.

"He's going to live at a nice big farm, with lots of other cats, where he can run and play and catch all the mice he can eat. Don't worry, honey. He'll have a happy life."

Ashley swallowed and wiped a tear from her cheek as she watched Daddy take the tiny kitten away.

SMOKEY THOUGHT HE WAS going for a ride. Another adventure, like exploring that cave of papers where Ashley had just taken him. He hoped Ashley would come, but he didn't mind being carried away by her daddy. Ashley's daddy had never been cruel to him. The cool outdoor air was fresh and his nose detected all kinds of strange, new smells.

The rumble of the pick-up truck's engine startled him, and he had to grip the upholstered seat with his tiny claws to keep from toppling over as the truck started to move. He took a few steps toward Daddy, but Daddy brushed him away. He tried to climb up the back of the seat so he could see out the window. They were going faster now. Trees covered with dormant kudzu, billboards, and telephone wires whizzed by in a blur. The motion of the truck made Smokey dizzy. With a squeaky meow, he crawled down from his perch and curled up in the fold of the seat.

Christmas music with a country twang played on the car radio. Daddy didn't talk to him like Ashley did.

They stopped abruptly. Smokey felt the truck lurch and stirred from his nap. Daddy opened the driver's side door and then leaned across the passenger seat. He yanked Smokey by the scruff of the neck, dragged him past the steering wheel, and tossed him onto the grass beside the road. "Bye, buddy," he said as he slammed the door and drove away.

Puzzled, Smokey watched the truck disappear in a cloud of dust, with Ashley's daddy inside. He sniffed at the tall, dry grass and then began chewing on a blade. It tasted bitter and he spit it out.

There was a big world to explore, and he was all alone.

THAT NIGHT, ASHLEY knelt beside her bed and said a prayer. After asking God to bless Mama and Daddy and all their family and friends, she asked Him, "Please watch over Smokey and help him find a good home."

She thought about the farm where Daddy had taken Smokey, where he had taken many other kittens that the pet store owner didn't want to buy. She had never been there, but when Daddy described it, it sounded like a magical place. There was a big barn full of hay that housed assorted animals. Smokey would meet the other cats, make friends, and learn to hunt rats with them.

She wondered if the family who lived there had children, and if they liked kittens. They were sure to love Smokey. Maybe Mama and Daddy would let her visit sometime.

THE NEXT MORNING, TEN miles south, Sharie filled a fresh bowl with dry cat food for Micky, her eight-year-old grey tabby. She stroked his big head as he plunged his face into the bowl. He gulped the kibble like a feral cat who didn't know when he'd get his next meal.

Ever since Micky's twin brother Myron had died of cancer last month, Micky did nothing but eat and sleep. He grew fatter by the day. The next bag of cat food she bought for Micky would have to be low calorie. If only he'd get more exercise.... They lived on a beautiful wooded lot with trees to climb and squirrels to chase, but Micky no longer showed any interest. He barely even played with his cat toys anymore.

She remembered when Micky and Myron were kittens, the last two left in their litter. Micky and Myron had been responsible for her meeting Andrew, the wonderful man who became her husband....

It had been a slow day at the PetSmart store, where Sharie's animal rescue group, Peachtree Humane, held pet adoptions. She and the other volunteers had started folding up the cages, ready to call it a day. She peered into the cage where Micky and Myron dozed in their pillow-like cat bed, wrapped around each other as if they were one cat. "Sorry, little guys. Maybe next week," she cooed.

"Cute," said a deep voice behind her. "What kind of cats are they?"

She turned her head to gaze into the warmest pair of brown eyes she'd ever seen. They reminded her of melted chocolate, and the visage they were attached to could have come from the silver screen.

"Domestic short hair." She smiled. "Just your common house cat. But they're darling, don't you agree?" She straightened and faced him. "Are you looking for a cat?"

His eyes swept from her to the cage containing the kittens. Micky and Myron had awakened and had started batting at him through the bars. "I was looking for a dog. I've never had a cat. Not sure what I'd do with it."

"Cats are much easier to care for." Sharie slipped into sales mode. "Is anyone in the family home during the day?" She noticed he wasn't wearing a wedding ring, and no children tagged after him, but that didn't necessarily mean anything.

He shook his head. "I live alone." His slender fingers danced with Myron's little paws through the cage bars. "I work long hours, and it would be nice to have a pet to come home to."

"You need a cat then," Sharie told him. "A dog can't be left alone that long. You'd always be watching the clock, having to dash home to let the dog out. Leave the cat with a clean litter box and full bowls of food and water, and he's good all week-end."

Her potential customer smiled as Myron sniffed his hand. "Can I hold him?"

"Sure." As Sharie reached into the cage to retrieve Myron, she brushed against the young man's shoulder. She caught a whiff of a pleasant, fresh-scented after-shave. "Let's go into the back room so we don't have to worry about the kitten escaping in the store."

The man pet Myron's head as he followed Sharie to the meet-and-greet room. "I'm Andrew, by the way."

"Sharie." She held the kitten close to her chest but tilted his face toward Andrew. "And this is Myron, although you're free to change his name after you adopt him."

"I don't know. I'd feel funny doing that. He's probably used to being called Myron."

"They adapt." Sharie glanced back at the cage where Micky pawed at the bars. "Want to take both kittens? They're brothers, and they play well together. They've never been separated." She flashed him her brightest smile. "Since you're gone all day, one kitten would be lonely. Two will keep each other company and out of trouble." She opened the door to the meet-and-greet room. "I can leave you two in here to get acquainted while I bring his brother."

Andrew laughed, more melodic than derisive. "Don't push it. Five minutes ago, I didn't know I'd even consider adopting a cat."

After a game of feather-fishing in the meet-and-greet room, Andrew was clearly smitten. Sharie moved in for the kill.

Myron curled up on Andrew's lap while Sharie explained in detail each form that had to be completed.

"I didn't realize adopting a cat was as complicated as buying a house," Andrew said with a grin.

"Almost like adopting a child," Sharie agreed, although she'd never adopted a child. She was just repeating what other pet adopters had told her.

In addition to copies of the adoption paperwork and Myron's vet records, Sharie gave Andrew a stack of brochures about caring for his new kitten: "Kitten-proof Your House." "What If Your Cat Won't Use the Litterbox?" "Cats and Claws." "How to Keep Your Kitten Healthy." "Why You Should Keep Your Cat Indoors."

Their hands grazed as Andrew took the materials. "Guess I have some reading to do."

Despite her best efforts, Sharie was unable to persuade Andrew to take Micky as well. Micky cried all night for his missing brother.

A few days later, Sharie saw an unfamiliar phone number pop up on her caller ID. She hesitated, then answered, hoping it wasn't a telemarketer.

A deep voice, vaguely familiar, asked, "Sharie Simpson? From the Peachtree Humane Society?"

"Yes." She tried to place the voice.

"Last weekend I adopted a kitten from you. Myron."

"Oh, Myron! How's he doing?" She remembered those mesmerizing brown eyes. That chiseled face. And the fact that stubborn man had broken up a bonded pair of brothers.

There was a pause. "Everything was fine until tonight. Now something's wrong."

Sharie's heart pounded. "What do you mean? What happened?"

"He's throwing up. He was fine, and then all of a sudden..."

"Maybe he ate something that didn't agree with him? What have you been feeding him?"

"Just the food you gave me with the adoption coupons. And a little milk."

"Milk?"

"He loves it."

Sharie sighed. "Cats drinking milk is a myth. Most of them are lactose intolerant. Especially with cow's milk."

He was silent. "What have I done?"

"How long has he been throwing up?"

"He just started. He hasn't ever done this before. Why would he drink milk if it makes him sick?"

Sharie switched the phone to her other ear. "Sometimes it takes a little while for the allergy to manifest itself."

"What should I do? Should I take him to the vet?"

"It's Sunday, and no one's open except the emergency clinic downtown." She wondered if Andrew could afford their fees. What if he decided to have the kitten euthanized rather than pay the bill? "What's he doing now?"

"He's quiet. Like he wants to go to sleep."

"Listen, Andrew, I think he'll be fine if you don't give him any more milk. Give him plenty of clean water and put out some dry kitten food for when his appetite comes back."

"You're sure? I'm worried about him." His voice trembled. "You don't think I should take him to the emergency clinic?"

Sharie looked at her watch. "Where do you live?" She hated to give advice over the phone that might be wrong. "I'm not a veterinarian, but I'm employed as a vet tech. I'd be happy to examine him and then we can decide if he needs to go to the emergency clinic."

"That would be wonderful." Relief rushed through Andrew's voice as he gave her the address.

Myron had almost completely recovered from his vomiting bout by the time Sharie arrived.

She picked up Myron and kissed him. "Your brother misses you." The kitten rewarded her with a weak purr. "Micky told me you have to get better."

"Sorry I dragged you out tonight," said Andrew. "I didn't think to ask if you were busy. It was just that..."

"You're a nervous new father." Sharie winked at him.

"Can I get you something to drink?"

They sipped hot chocolate by the fire and talked for hours. They discussed their jobs and families and their favorite music. Sharie told him how she'd been involved in animal rescue since high school and that she was studying to become a veterinarian.

"How can you foster?" Andrew asked. "Don't you get attached?"

"Of course." Sharie gazed into the fire, thinking of the many kittens she had loved and cared for over the years. "But the goal is to find them a good home. When you've made the perfect match, you learn to let them go."

He looked fondly at Myron, who had snuggled into Sharie's lap. "Still, it must be hard."

"I know I can't keep them all. And getting one adopted makes room for another. One more life I can save."

The embers died; it was time to leave. But Myron had fallen asleep on her lap, and she hated to disturb him.

When Myron stirred and contorted his body into a contented stretch, kneading the air with his tiny claws, Sharie took the opportunity to lift him off her lap and place him in Andrew's arms. "I think he'll be fine. Give me a call if he starts throwing up again."

He walked her to the door. "Thank you."

As she looked into his chocolate eyes, she thought he might kiss her. But he didn't.

The next weekend at PetSmart, a family took Micky into the meet-and-greet room. "We love him," the mother told Sharie. "Let's do it."

Sharie gave the woman the pre-adoption questionnaire and put Micky back into his cage to wait while his new family completed their paperwork. As she latched the cage door, she bumped squarely into Andrew.

"Oh, good, he's still here." He pointed at Micky. "You were right. Myron needs a companion. I'd like to adopt his brother."

"Here you go." The woman handed Sharie her completed application and bent to pet Micky through the bars of his cage.

Andrew looked at Sharie in alarm. "Someone's adopting him?"

Sharie nodded. If only Andrew had arrived earlier.... On the other hand, she'd tried to talk him into taking both kittens when he adopted Myron last weekend. It served him right for not listening to her.

Andrew watched, crestfallen, as the woman tickled Micky through the cage bars. He put his hand inside the cage as well, and Micky turned his attention to Andrew, started to lick his fingers.

Sharie smiled, thinking that maybe Andrew carried the scent of Myron, and Micky recognized it. She studied the preadoption questionnaire. "Ma'am," she addressed Micky's potential adopter. "I see you have two German Shepherds. Have they been around cats?"

The woman gave Sharie a blank look which made Sharie uncomfortable.

"Micky is afraid of big dogs." Sharie wasn't sure this was true; she didn't own a dog, and Micky never spent any time around one. Her only proof was an episode a few weeks earlier, when a PetSmart customer had walked his Great Dane too close to the cat cages, and Micky, along with Myron and several other kittens, had gone berserk.

The woman's children were already fawning over another litter of kittens in a cage at the end of the table. Sharie pointed to them. "Those kittens live with a large dog in their foster home so they would probably be more comfortable around your dog. Do you want to meet some of those before you make up your mind? It might be a better fit for your family."

The woman agreed, and just like that Micky went home with Andrew.

A week passed and Andrew called again. Sharie recognized his voice this time. "Is something wrong with one of the boys?"

"They're doing great," Andrew assured her. "I could watch them play together for hours. They're hilarious!"

"I'm glad." Sharie waited. She could feel her heartbeat quicken, even though she knew there was nothing wrong with her beloved former foster kittens.

"I think they miss you." Andrew's voice was soft. "In fact, Micky told me so."

She chuckled.

"They asked if you could come visit them sometime."

"Well..."

"I make a mean lasagna."

"I love lasagna." *And I love a man who can cook*, thought Sharie.

"How's tomorrow night?"

"What can I bring?"

Three months later, they got engaged. Six months after that, Andrew and Sharie were married. They didn't have human children but Micky and Myron were their babies.

Myron's death was a crushing reminder of the differences in their life spans.

ANDREW HONKED THE HORN, and Sharie hurried out to the garage so she wouldn't keep him waiting. Today, they were driving to the north side of Atlanta to join friends for a Christmas party.

"Micky needs a friend," Sharie said, as they exited their circular driveway. "He's lonely."

Andrew sighed. They'd had this conversation before. "I think he likes being the only cat. Now he gets all your attention."

"If Myron were the survivor, I might agree with you." She opened her compact and checked her lipstick. "But Micky's always loved other cats." They'd watched a movie on television last night, and a cat had been meowing on screen. When Micky heard it, his ears had perked up, and he'd started searching behind the television for the other cat.

They headed north on the two-lane highway, past forests and cow pastures and a horse farm. Just before they reached the railroad tracks, Sharie caught a glimpse of something white moving in the tall grass by the edge of the road. "Honey, that looks like a kitten."

"You have kittens on the brain. Everything looks like a kitten to you," Andrew replied as they drove across the railroad tracks.

THE FLEAS BIT SMOKEY faster than he could flick their tiny black bodies off his thin white fur. His infected eye oozed, and gnats flew around the discharge. He ventured onto the pavement to escape the tall grass, which was full of bugs, but then a big silver car zoomed by and sent him back to the safety of the ditch.

On the other side of the ditch lay a barbed wire fence. Smokey climbed up the incline and peered through the fence. He spied a farmhouse in the distance, and a faded red wooden barn closer by. Smokey crawled through the fence and started toward the farmhouse. His stomach growled with hunger. His mouth was parched. Houses meant people, and people meant food.

A huge black creature blocked his path. Hooves threatened to crush him as the animal bellowed, "Moo!" Smokey scampered back through the fence, abandoning his quest to reach the farmhouse.

When was Daddy coming back? He'd been gone for hours; it was past lunchtime. Smokey was ready to go home. Back to Ashley, back to his littermates. Their tiny cage was better than this.

SMOKEY DOZED IN THE shade of a privet bush. Rustling grass caught his attention. A tiny gray animal scampered past him. He'd seen his mother catch one once, and she had eaten it.

Quick as a lightning flash, Smokey lunged after the mouse. His claws grazed its tail, but the mouse slipped away. Smokey was too weak to catch it, and too tired to run after it. The hope of dinner was gone. The grass he had swallowed earlier made his stomach hurt. Choking, he felt a wad of grass and fur well up in his throat.

AS THE SUN SET BELOW the horizon, Andrew and Sharie drove south down the highway toward home. The Christmas party had been fun; many of their friends from the old neighborhood had attended. They'd shared pictures of their trips and their houses and their families. Sharie had passed around photos of Micky and Myron, and everyone had sympathized with her about Myron's untimely passing.

"Are you going to get another cat?" someone asked. "To keep Micky company."

Sharie and Andrew looked at each other. He shook his head. "It's too soon."

"Andrew loved Myron so much, and he doesn't think another cat can replace him. But some day, he'll want to save another life," Sharie replied.

Andrew gave her a grim smile, and his eyes watered.

After the party, they'd gone shopping at the outlet mall and purchased holiday gifts for most everyone on their list. They were exhausted.

Smokey sat at the edge of the highway, wondering whether to cross. Cars sped by infrequently; he could probably make it to the other side before the next vehicle passed. There were not as many fleas close to the road as there were in the weeds. Maybe life would be better on the other side.

Light from the setting sun filtered through the tall grass and reflected off Smokey's white coat, forming a halo around him. As Sharie looked out the windshield, she glimpsed the shape of a tiny white kitten against the green grass. "There's a kitten by the side of the road! This time I'm sure of it. Andrew, turn around! What is that kitten doing way out here, all by itself?"

"Where?" Obeying, Andrew took the next turnout and headed back in the other direction, driving slowly as Sharie pressed her face against the car window, searching for the kitten.

"Stop!" Sharie commanded, as she spotted Smokey scampering up the incline toward a barbed wire fence. Andrew braked and Sharie opened the passenger door. "Here, kitty," she called softly, jumping out of the car. The ground was uneven and the tall grass scratched her legs through her pantyhose.

At the sound of Sharie's voice, Smokey stopped running away. People. Maybe they would feed him. He raced back toward Sharie's open arms.

Sharie picked up Smokey and cuddled him against her chest. "Oh, you poor kitty," she clucked, stroking his thin fur. She clutched him tightly and climbed back into the car. "Look Andrew, he's part Siamese! Isn't he beautiful? Oh, those clear blue eyes!" Smokey's little heart pounded and he purred loudly. "How could someone abandon such a beautiful kitten?"

Andrew gave her a sideways glance. "He is kind of cute."

Sharie closed the car door, attached her seat belt, and settled Smokey onto her lap. "I'll give him a bath as soon as we get home." She kissed Smokey on the top of his head. "Oh, he's trembling! He must be starving!"

"What's Micky going to do?" Andrew asked.

"Micky will get used to him. He'll like having a little brother," Sharie replied. "We'll keep them separate at first until they get used to each other. Learn their smells. Gradual introduction." She spoke the advice she'd given to many adoptive families who were adding a new pet to their menagerie.

She held Smokey firmly but gently as he squirmed to investigate the unfamiliar car. "Oh, he has an eye infection. I'll take him to the clinic with me tomorrow. I'm sure he'll need shots, too."

Andrew sighed and smiled at his wife. "Looks like we're getting a new family member."

Smokey purred as the car moved.

Andrew turned the car around and headed home. Smokey had never met these people, but he had a good feeling about them. He knew they would be his forever family.

About the Author

B io:
Sharon Marchisello is the author of *Going Home* (Sunbury Press, 2014) a murder mystery inspired by her mother's battle with Alzheimer's disease. Her second mystery, *Secrets of the Galapagos*, will be released later this year. An active member of Atlanta Sisters in Crime, she contributed a short story to their 1999 anthology, *Mystery, Atlanta Style*. Her latest short story, "The Wrong Coffee Shop", can be found in the 2018 Darkhouse Books anthology, *Shhhh... Murder!* Sharon earned a Masters in Professional Writing from the University of Southern California and has written travel articles, corporate training manuals, and book reviews, many of which have appeared in the Killer Nashville online magazine. She also writes a blog about personal finance, *Countdown to Financial Fitness*, and self-published a personal finance book in 2018, *Live Well, Grow Wealth*.

Social Media:
facebook.com/SLMarchisello/
https://twitter.com/SLMarchisello
https://smarchisello.wordpress.com/
https://www.goodreads.com/author/show/
4297807.Sharon_Marchisello

https://www.linkedin.com/in/sharonmarchisello/

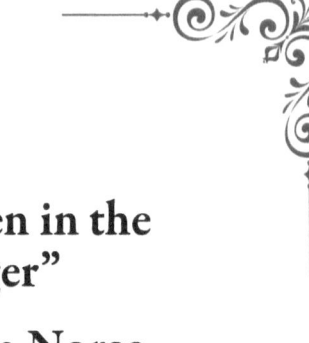

"The Kitten in the Manger"
By Isabella Norse

HOLLY SHIFTED THE BOX of gingerbread cookies to one hand, and raised the other to knock on the heavy wooden door decorated with a galvanized metal reindeer, and firmly tamped down the gigantic rush of butterflies flitting about her belly. What had she been thinking when she agreed to attend a Christmas party with Jeremy as their second date? Parties had never been her thing. Oh well, what was done was done. She'd just have to make the most of it and hope their budding relationship could withstand the strain of her social awkwardness. She realized she was still standing there, hand poised to knock on the door. "Get a grip girl. Just knock," she whispered, giving herself a much needed pep talk.

Just as she drew her hand back, she heard a faint mewling and glanced around for the source. There, huddled on the corner of the doormat, was a tiny light gray kitten shivering in the cold. "Oh, you poor thing!" She looked around but didn't see the mother or any other kittens anywhere. "I can't just leave you out here. You're coming with me." She stooped and scooped up the kitten with her free hand then realized she had left herself nothing to announce her presence with. So, she raised one foot and kicked gently on the brass kick plate at the base of the door.

A deep, throaty bark issued from the depths of the house in response. "Coming!" Jeremy pitched his voice to be heard over the canine cacophony. The door opened, framing Jeremy and a tail-wagging Bassett-something mix against the twinkling lights of the Christmas tree behind them. It was a picture worthy of a Christmas card or romance novel cover. "Hi!" Jeremy smiled at Holly and her heart fluttered. His lopsided grin got her every time, as did the peppering of silver hair in his short beard and at his temples. "Come on in." He stepped aside giving her room to enter, coaxing the dog back as he did so. "This is Buster, my wireless doorbell." He reached down and ruffled the dog's ears earning him a doggie grin. "I'm running a few minutes late, as usual. Make yourself at home while I finish a couple of things and then we'll head out."

"Hello to you too." Holly grinned at Jeremy, hoping her expression wasn't as goofy as she felt. No need to let him know the full impact he had on her. She didn't want to scare him away. Shifting her attention to the dog she added, "Nice to meet you Buster."

Buster stood on his hind legs and pawed at Holly's coat. Jeremy looked mortified. "I'm so sorry. Buster, what has gotten into you?"

"Maybe this has something to do with it." Holly held out the hand containing the trembling kitten. "Is it yours? It was just sitting on the doormat. It's a miracle I didn't step on it, it was so still."

"No, I've never seen this kitten before." Jeremy took the baby from Holly's hand and examined it carefully. "Where did you come from? You don't look old enough to be away from your mama yet, little one." He looked up at Holly. "We need to get this baby warmed up and fed as soon as possible. Are you willing to help?"

"Absolutely. Anything for an animal in need. Just tell me what you want me to do."

"Well, let's start with freeing up your hands. I'm assuming the box is the cookies you said you would make so, how about placing them on the kitchen counter." He nodded to the appropriate doorway. "Just make sure to push the box back from the edge. Buster may be short but he has a sweet tooth and no shame. Then, you can hang your coat on the rack next to the door."

Holly did as instructed and then returned to Jeremy's side where he continued to check the kitten over. "I don't see any obvious injuries but this baby is thin and too young to go without food for too long." He took Holly's elbow and guided her to the fireplace which contained a fire blazing merrily behind a steel and beveled glass screen. He handed her the kitten. "Have a seat on one of those cushions. I'll be right back." He disappeared around the corner at a trot.

Holly pulled a floor cushion as close to the fireplace as she could stand, then sat and clutched the kitten to her chest. She stroked the tiny body, hoping the combined warmth of the fire and her body heat would ease the poor thing's trembling.

"There, there." She crooned and whispered to the tiny feline, rocking it as she would a human baby.

As Holly waited for Jeremy's return, she gazed around at her surroundings, getting to know him a little better through the things he chose to surround himself with. The walls were painted a no-nonsense beige, while the furnishings were a dark brown as were the heavy wooden shelves lining the walls. However, it was the accessories that made her smile. The cushion she sat on and what appeared to be a matching bed for Buster were of a cheerful red and black buffalo plaid, as was the throw draped over the back of the couch. The more she looked the more splashes of color she found. The mantel was decorated with an artificial evergreen garland dotted with white lights and pinecones. Now that the chaos of her arrival had faded she realized that Christmas music was playing softly over an unseen stereo system.

Buster plodded over, his toenails clicking against the hardwood floor, and sat next to Holly, stretching out his muzzle for a sniff. She held her free hand out to him and was rewarded with the swipe of a wet tongue across her knuckles. He eased closer, nosing toward the kitten in her hand. Holly didn't know what to do. She didn't think Buster would hurt the kitten but she really didn't know him and the small cat was already terrified.

"Here." She jumped, not realizing that Jeremy had returned and knelt next to her. He held out a well-worn hand towel. "Wrap the baby up in this. It's fresh from the dryer and it's still warm." He saw Buster straining toward the kitten, eager to investigate the new arrival. "Don't worry about him. Buster won't hurt the kitten; he loves babies of all species. I call him my nanny dog. He helps me care for all of the babies I foster."

"Wait, what?" Holly quickly swaddled the kitten forming a towel "purrito" with only a small gray face sticking out. "You're a foster dad?"

Jeremy plopped down on to the floor next to Holly. "Yes, of a sort. I foster kittens for Unconditional Love animal shelter. As a matter of fact, my last group of fosters just moved to the main facility so they can be put up for adoption. I've spent most of the day cleaning my foster room and getting it ready for the next batch of arrivals, whenever that may be."

Buster whined, still straining to reach the kitten. Jeremy laughed. "Hold the kitten out for him to check. He's not going to settle down until he assesses the situation." Holly flicked her glance between the man and the dog then shrugged and extended the hand containing the kitten, prepared to snatch it back if needed. She needn't have worried.

Buster nuzzled the kitten, sniffing it carefully before swiping its face with his tongue. Instead of freaking out at the attentions of the larger animal, the kitten relaxed, sagging into Holly's hand.

"Well, would you look at that? That's the most relaxed this poor baby has been since I picked it up."

"I told you. Buster has the magic touch. Now, if the three of you are doing okay, I'm going to get something for the little one to eat." Jeremy pushed to his feet and disappeared into the kitchen where Holly could hear cabinets opening and closing and the running of water.

"I'm not sure if this baby is old enough to be weaned, so I thought we'd start with a bottle of milk replacer." Jeremy held up a bottle of milky liquid when he returned. "Have you ever bottle fed a kitten?" When Holly shook her head he held his hands out. "Well, then why don't you let me do the honors?"

Holly handed over the kitten and watched in fascination as Jeremy unwrapped it, feeling it carefully. "First things first. We don't want to feed the baby until it has warmed up. A kitten can't regulate its own body temperature and feeding it when it's cold could lower its temperature into dangerous territory. However, you and Buster have done an admirable job and I think this little one is warm enough to feed." He carefully positioned the baby on its belly and began encouraging it to drink. It took a couple of false starts but the kitten quickly latched on and began drinking with gusto.

Jeremy scooted around until he could lean back against a recliner and stretched his long legs out in front of him. Buster positioned himself at Jeremy's side, watching to make sure everything was handled properly. He smiled down at the kitten and then turned his attention back to Holly. "It seems you've been hiding your light under a bushel so to speak. The way you swaddled this kitten tells me this isn't your first time at the feline rodeo."

"Not hardly. I've had pets—mainly cats—as long as I can remember. I tried doing the foster thing too but I was a complete and utter foster failure. Now I take in senior cats in need of a home and love on them for whatever time they have left."

"Wow." Jeremy looked at her with what seemed to be a heightened sense of appreciation. "That's got to be hard."

"It is, but there is nothing I'd rather do. Some of the cats have outlived their owners. Others have been dumped by owners no longer willing to care for them when they start showing signs of old age. And don't even get me started on what I think of people like that, I try not to use that kind of language. Whatever their circumstances, I just want these cats to know love and comfort for whatever time they have left." She drew a shuddering breath and blinked back tears. "Each of them leaves a hole in my heart when their time comes to an end but..." She shrugged, words failing her.

"You're a pretty special woman." Holly could almost hear the "click" when Jeremy's eyes met hers. Her breath caught in her chest. She wasn't quite sure what had just happened but something most definitely had shifted between them.

"Thanks." She blushed. "You're no slouch yourself. There aren't enough people willing to do what you do."

The praise fest was broken by an indignant squeak. Jeremy laughed when he saw that the kitten had lost its grip on the nipple and now had milk splattered on its face. Before he could react, Buster stepped in as clean-up crew and licked the kitten's face clean. "Now on to the less savory aspect of bottle feeding." He used the towel to wipe its genitals, encouraging it to pee and poop. That done, he wadded the towel up, pushed to his feet and headed to the back of the house again only to return with the kitten wrapped in a small piece of fleece.

"I'm glad you found this baby. She's extremely thin and dirty. I don't think she's had a mama taking care of her for a while."

"How do you think it wound up on your stairs?"

Jeremy shrugged. "I put a food dish out for the neighborhood strays. The moms bring their babies by to teach them where to find food. A mom could have brought her baby and then something happened to her or someone who knows I help animals could have left it. There's really no way to know for sure. He stroked the kitten's head. "I don't think she would have made it if we hadn't found her until after the party."

"The party!" Holly jerked upright from her lounging position. "I completely forgot. We're going to be late."

"It's okay. I've already texted my friends to let them know that we'll either be late or not there at all."

"I'm so sorry. I didn't mean to mess up your—I mean our—plans."

"No apology necessary. My friends are used to this sort of behavior from me. They know my heart for animals. I assure you, it won't be the first time I've canceled because of a kitten crisis. I also have the local vet on speed dial just in case we need to take her in."

"You're a good man." Holly realized she could fall for this guy hard. It was time to steer the conversation back onto safer grounds. "You keep saying 'she'. Is it a girl?"

"It's always hard to know for sure when they're so young, but I'm pretty sure this one is a girl. In honor of the Christmas season, I think I'm going to call her Angel. What do you think?"

"I think Angel is a perfect name." Holly shifted, pulling her knees up and resting her chin on them. "So, what do we do now?"

"Well, I want to keep an eye on Angel to make sure she's doing okay before we head out, if we decide to do so. How about I show you the rest of the house? You can see how a crazy cat daddy sets up his foster room." Jeremy stood, tucked the sleeping kitten into the crook of his elbow and held his free hand out to Holly.

Holly placed her hand in his and let him pull her to her feet. She stood, her face mere inches from his. They were almost the same height. It would be so easy to stretch out just a bit and kiss him. Before she could act on the impetuous thought, Buster pushed his way between them.

Jeremy laughed. "I think someone's jealous." He mock-scolded his dog. "We need to work on your timing big guy. You really know how to spoil a moment."

Spoil a moment? Had Jeremy been feeling the same way? Holly ducked her head under the pretense of petting Buster and peered up at Jeremy through her lashes. He was watching her, only the dimple in his left cheek giving away his amusement.

"Shall we get this tour underway? If it's okay with Buster, that is."

Buster woofed under his breath and wagged his tail, wiggling his entire rear end in agreement.

"I'll take that as a yes. Follow me." Jeremy still held Holly's hand and used it to lead her down the hall. He stopped at the first room on the left. "This is my office."

Holly glanced in and cringed. It seemed that Mr. Potentially Perfect had a major flaw. The room was in a complete state of chaos. "Wow. This is so... different from the living area and kitchen."

"Uh oh. Please don't tell me you're a neat freak?"

"Okay. I won't tell you. Just ignore any eye twitches or other tics that may manifest in the next few minutes." Holly took a deep breath and peered into the office. "You told me that you work from home. What exactly do you do?"

"I'm a freelance web site designer. I specialize in helping small businesses and non-profit organizations."

"Impressive." Holly grinned at him. "You, sir, are full of surprises. What's next?"

"Next up is the laundry room. But, I'll warn you. It's a bit of a disaster area right now too."

"Actually, I was expecting far worse." Both the top-of-the-line washer and dryer were running and a small mound of towels waited their turn. Metal shelves filled with bins lined one wall. Each shelf was neatly labeled. "This looks like something I would do. A place for everything and everything in its place."

"Organization doesn't come naturally to me, but I can learn." Jeremy pointed at the shelves. "Once I began fostering entire litters of kittens it was important that I be able to find what I needed when I needed it, and not have to spend several minutes searching." He stepped back into the hall and quickly closed the door to the room at the end. "That's the master bedroom. You don't need to see that."

"Oh?" Holly arched one brow.

"That's where I shoved all of the things I removed from the living area before you came over. I didn't want you to think I'm a *complete* slob. And, I'm not. I just don't mind if my house looks... lived in. Anyway," he led her to the next door on the other side of the hall. "This is the foster room. It's pretty bare now but when I'm fostering it's full of play pens, cat trees, toys, litterboxes, food dishes, and of course, kittens."

"So, do you just foster orphaned kittens or moms and kittens?"

"I've done both but orphaned kittens are my specialty. Not everyone has the time to devote to bottle-feeding babies and I do. So, I guess it's sort of a match made in heaven." He nodded to the last door before they re-entered the living area. "That's the bathroom, or powder room if you prefer." Once the tour concluded he checked on Angel again. "She seems to be warming up nicely. Her nose and ears are a bit pinker too. That makes me very happy." He cocked his head before addressing Holly. "Would you be too upset if we skipped the party? I'm not comfortable leaving Angel at this point."

"Not at all." Holly couldn't hide the relief that flooded through her. She blushed when she saw Jeremy's expression. "I'm sure your friends are wonderful people and I look forward to meeting them. However, parties and I don't mix well. I think I hide it fairly well most of the time but I'm actually kind of shy. When I'm in a party situation all of my social anxieties flare up. Who should I talk to? What should we talk about? Am I saying too much or not enough? I wind up being that person in the corner playing with the host's pets. If they don't have any pets, I just stand around awkwardly trying to figure out what to do with my hands until it's socially acceptable for me to leave." She shrugged. "What can I say? I'm loads of fun. I probably should have warned you when you invited me but... I really wanted to see you again and was willing to take my chances. I figured having you there to make the introductions and steer the conversations would make things easier." The heat level in her cheeks rose a few more degrees.

Jeremy laughed. "I guess I did kind of throw you into the deep end of the dating pool by inviting you to a party with all of my friends so soon." He gave her a quick one-armed hug. "I appreciate your honesty and the fact that you were such a good sport about it." He searched the room. "Ah ha!" He took Angel to the nativity scene in the corner and placed her in the manger with the figure of baby Jesus. "I don't think He will mind sharing. Now I'll be able to keep an eye on her while we're in the kitchen." Buster wandered over and sniffed the newcomer from stem to stern, gave the top of her head a careful lick and then plopped down beside the nativity scene with a sigh. "Buster will also let me know if anything requires my attention." He leaned over and stroked the dog lovingly. "He's the ultimate Good Boy."

"So, why does a man who obviously loves cats so much not have one of his own?"

"I did." He pointed to the fireplace mantel. "See the cat statue? It's actually an urn containing the ashes of my cat Max."

Holly walked over for a closer look. "You had your cat cremated?"

"Of course." Jeremy moved to her side and ran his fingertips over the figurine. "There are city ordinances about burying pets in the backyard. Even if there weren't, what if I were to move? I couldn't leave my best friend behind."

Holy cow. Holly didn't think she could stand it if this guy became any more awesome. "I totally get it. I've had several pets cremated myself. Most people think it's weird."

"Not in my book." The corners of Jeremy's eyes crinkled as he smiled. "Have I ever told you that I think you're pretty cool?"

Holly ducked her head. "No, you haven't. And, thanks. So are you." She chuckled. "So, what are the members of the local mutual admiration society—meaning us—going to do about food since we won't be dining with your friends?"

"My kitchen is usually pretty well stocked. Why don't we see what we can come up with?"

They moved to the kitchen where Holly waited for Jeremy to take the lead, since she had no idea what he considered "well stocked" or where anything might be. She didn't want to just start rummaging through his cabinets willy-nilly. After an extended pause she asked, "So, where should we start?"

"Do you like vegetable soup?"

"Homemade? You better believe it."

Jeremy opened the refrigerator door. "Well then, you're in luck. I just made a fresh batch yesterday. All we have to do is heat it up." He removed the container of soup from the fridge, and placed it on the counter so he could begin the search for a pot to warm it up in.

"Did I see beer in the fridge?"

"You did." Jeremy looked at Holly with heightened interest. "Don't tell me you like beer."

"Sometimes. I was just thinking, if you have all the ingredients, I can whip up some beer bread to go with the soup. It'll take about an hour and a half to get it prepped and baked though."

"I don't mind waiting. It'll give us a chance to get to know each other better. I think you can tell a lot about a person based on how well they share a small kitchen."

"Oh really? I don't think I've ever seen that in one of those 'Is This the One?' quizzes."

Jeremy finally located his Dutch oven, freed it from the confines of the cabinet, and stepped around Holly to place it on the stove before retrieving the container of chilled soup. "There are quizzes about that sort of thing?"

"Oh yeah. Online and in women's magazines. I personally don't put much stock in them though. I think I'm the only one who can determine if a relationship or person is right for me."

Jeremy glanced at her over his shoulder, his eyes dancing with mischief. "How am I doing?"

"So far so good." Before Holly could continue, a bark issued from the living room. She shooed Jeremy away. "You go check on Buster and Angel while I scout out ingredients and get started on the bread."

Holly had just started mixing ingredients when Jeremy returned carrying the kitten and a fresh bottle. Buster trailed behind him, not willing to let his new feline charge out of his sight. "All is well. Angel had woken up and was a bit fidgety. I'm going to see if I can get her to eat again. At this age, frequent feedings are important since she can't take in much at one go. It's even more important now since we don't know how long she might have gone without." He seated himself on one of the stools at the island dinette, placed Angel in his lap, and began the feeding process again. The kitten latched on quicker this time and began suckling, her eyes closed in concentration. Eating, it seemed, was very serious business.

"You're running low on flour but I found some cornmeal, so I changed things up a bit. Instead of beer bread, I'm preparing cornbread. I hope you don't mind—especially since it's going in the oven now." Holly put her words into action and slid the pan into the oven before moving the dirty bowls and utensils to the sink.

"I love cornbread. Maybe you can make beer bread for me some other time. I've never had it." He stroked Angel with one finger, his expression softening as he watched her. "I think I'm going to keep her. Max's death was hard on me but it also left an empty place in my heart. I think Angel might just be the kitten that can fill it." Buster woofed his approval, putting his front paws on Jeremy's leg as he checked to make sure his kitten wasn't in any distress. Angel ignored him and continued to drink.

Holly smiled at the trio as she began filling the sink with hot water and added a splash of dish detergent. "I think that's a wonderful idea. The three of you make a cute family."

"Thanks." He nodded at the sink. "You don't have to do that. Just pop them in the dishwasher."

"It's okay. I don't mind. I actually like washing dishes by hand. I find it relaxing. Besides, it gives me something to do while you kitten sit."

"In that case, knock yourself out." He smiled down at the kitten in his lap. "I think she's almost finished. She's starting to slow down. I'm surprised she has eaten as much as she has. Poor thing must be famished." He put the bottle down and used the corner of the towel to clean Angel's face. "You're a messy eater kiddo." He cocked his head and studied his new friend. "You know, I think she may actually be white instead of gray." He held her up and turned her to face Holly. "I made a clean spot with the towel and her fur looks lighter there."

Holly squinted over her shoulder. "You may be right. Either way, she's a pretty little girl. What color are her eyes? Or have they changed yet?"

Jeremy turned the kitten back to face him. "What color are your eyes, hmmm?" He adopted the universal higher-pitched tone most people automatically use when speaking to a baby of any species. "They're still mostly blue but look like they're just starting to change. I think they'll probably be green when they're done. If so, you're going to be a knock-out aren't you, little girl?" He laughed. "Now that her tummy is full, she's falling asleep. So, if you will excuse us, I'll finish her ablutions, help her go potty, and then tuck her in for another nap."

"Have fun!" Holly turned her attention to the dishes and made short work of them, humming along to the Christmas music still playing on the stereo. She had just finished up and turned her attention to the soup which was starting to simmer when Jeremy returned, drying his hands on a paper towel.

"Angel is once again napping in her makeshift bed and Buster is on stand-by." He leaned against the doorframe. "You look quite at home in the kitchen." He blanched, his expression horrified. "Oh, I'm so sorry. I didn't mean that in a Neanderthal a-woman's-place-is-in-the-kitchen sort of way. I just meant that you seem happy here. Peaceful even."

"No offense taken." She glanced up and smiled before resuming her stirring. "I guess I am. It wasn't always this way. I never learned to cook when I was young. Even when I married, it was a struggle. Cooking didn't come naturally to me. Then, once I was widowed, it got worse. I hated trying to cook for one and just didn't see the point. Eventually though, I got tired of eating out all the time and started teaching myself to cook." She laughed. "I watched a lot of cooking shows and even tried a few of those meal-kit plans. More than one culinary experiment went in the trash. But, eventually food and I stopped being enemies and came to a truce. Now, I don't mind getting in the kitchen and throwing together a meal, or a dessert." She nodded at the box of cookies on the counter. "This is the first time I've successfully made gingerbread."

Jeremy stepped on the foot pedal to open the trashcan and dropped in his paper towel. "You're a widow? I'm sorry. That must have been hard."

"It was." Holly gazed sightlessly into the soup pot as she stirred, then turned back to Jeremy with a bittersweet smile. "But, life goes on. You grieve and slowly you heal and learn how to live with the new normal." She chuckled. "That's probably why I was such a foster failure. At that point in my life, I couldn't bear to say goodbye to anyone else—not even cats. But, it was probably for the best. My fur-kids and their unconditional love helped me heal. It didn't matter to them if I was having a bad day, if I was sad or angry. No matter what, they just loved me through it. And now, I'm looking forward to the rest of my life and seeing what exciting new adventures lie ahead." She paused and checked the timer on her phone. "The cornbread will be ready in a couple of minutes. Why don't you grab plates, bowls, and utensils? We'll just serve from here."

"Sounds good." Jeremy did as instructed as Holly gave the soup one last stir then removed the golden brown cornbread from the oven and sliced it. Once their bowls and plates were filled, they sat side-by-side at the bar.

"Oops. We forgot drinks." Jeremy hopped to his feet. "What would you like?"

"Just water for me please."

Jeremy returned with two glasses of water and they tucked into their meals with enthusiasm.

"Mmmm." Holly closed her eyes and sighed in bliss. "This soup is wonderful. You're not such a bad cook yourself."

"Thank you." Jeremy beamed with pleasure. "Like you said, cooking for one is hard. The slow cooker is my best friend. I like being able to toss in a whole bunch of ingredients in the morning and then just let it do its thing all day. By the time I'm ready for dinner, everything is good to go. Then, I can live off the leftovers for a few days. Every now and then I'll mix up a batch of soup or something similar and freeze it for an easy meal later."

"That method certainly came in handy today." Holly unabashedly used a hunk of cornbread to sop up the last of the broth from her soup and popped it into her mouth.

"I'm glad you like it." Jeremy pushed to his feet. "I think I'll have some more." Just as he began refilling his bowl, Buster let out a woof from the other room. "Oops, guess I better go see what's going on."

"What? No." Holly pushed to her feet and placed her dirty dishes in the sink. "You eat. I'll check on the animals."

Jeremy had just finished slathering his second slice of cornbread with butter when Holly returned with a squirming handful of kitten. "I think someone has caught up on her sleep—at least temporarily—and is ready to explore. Where do you keep your cat toys?"

"Check the shelves in the laundry room. All of the bins are labeled. Help yourself to whatever you think she might like."

"I can do that." She gave him a smile. "Take your time finishing. It's been a while since I've had a kitten to play with so I'll enjoy spending some time with her."

Jeremy took Holly at her word. She kept a running conversation with both Angel and Buster as she went down the hall, her voice fading with the distance. Her words were joined with the sound of jingle bells as she returned to the living area. He smiled at the sound of her laughter as she scattered toys across the hardwood floor for Angel to check out.

Holly was vaguely aware of Jeremy puttering around the kitchen but her attention was focused on Angel. The kitten was still at the adorable wobbly stage where her attempts to pounce on toys were just as likely to make her land on her nose as they were to actually make contact with the toy target. "Oof," she grunted as Buster plopped down beside her, leaning his not inconsiderable weight against her. She turned her attentions to the dog, stroking his silky ears. "So, does this nearness mean I've been accepted?" He responded with the swipe of his tongue across her cheek.

"That's a 'yes' in case you were wondering." Jeremy exited the kitchen carrying a tray. "I hope you like hot cocoa." He stepped carefully, watching for Angel, as he inched his way across the room to join Holly in front of the fireplace where he sat the tray on the hearth.

"I love chocolate in pretty much any form, including hot cocoa." Holly reached eagerly for a steaming mug topped with a generous dollop of whipped cream. "Oh, and you brought my cookies too." Her cheeks warmed with pleasure. "I hope you like them. Hey!" Buster shoved his muzzle toward the tray, jostling the arm holding her mug. "Easy there big guy." She sat her mug on the hearth and grabbed a napkin from the tray, wiping the cocoa from her fingers.

"Buster, sit." Jeremy commanded.

Buster sat, whining.

"Sorry about that. Are you okay?" He turned his attention to Holly.

"I'm fine. It just sloshed on my hand. No harm done." She wiggled her fingers as evidence. "I'm assuming that Buster thinks he should have some cocoa as well?"

"It's probably the gingerbread. He's still trying to convince me he needs people food from time to time."

"Can dogs have gingerbread?"

"No." Jeremy shook his head as he bit the head off a gingerbread man. "Ginger itself isn't bad for dogs but some of the other spices like nutmeg and anise are so, no cookies for Buster."

"I'm sorry Buster." Holly leaned forward to pet him. "If it's okay with your daddy, I'll see if I can find a dog-safe gingerbread recipe and make you some cookies of your very own."

"You'd do that for him?"

"Of course. Why wouldn't I?"

"It's just the sort of thing a lot of people wouldn't even think to do." Jeremy cocked his head, his dimple reappearing. "Thank you."

"You're welcome."

Buster gave up his attempts at winning cookies and turned his attention back to Angel, licking her each time she came close enough. He was in his element and began wagging his tail which instantly became Angel's toy of choice. She swatted and pounced at the wiggling object not seeming to mind when it knocked her over or slid her across the floor. Eventually, she fell asleep with her front legs wrapped around Buster's still swishing tail.

Jeremy laughed as he picked her up and placed her in his lap. "Typical baby. I'm always amazed at how a kitten can fall asleep in the middle of playing, frequently in what looks like an extremely uncomfortable position."

"I think she's happy here." Holly softly stroked the sleeping kitten's head with one finger. "I'm glad I found her and that you were equipped to take her in—and willing to do so."

"Me too." Jeremy reached out and squeezed Holly's fingers. "Some things are just meant to be." He twined his fingers through hers. "I'm glad we didn't go to the party. I've enjoyed spending time together, just the two of us." He glanced at Buster and Angel. "Well, more like the four of us."

"Me too." Holly glanced at the time on her phone. "I guess all good things must come to an end. I really should be getting home. I don't want to wear out my welcome."

"You're in no danger of doing that but, can I ask for one favor before you go?"

"Sure. What do you need?"

Jeremy transferred Angel from his lap to Holly's. "Will you hold her while I get her next bottle ready? After that play session, I'm sure she'll be famished when she wakes up."

"Gladly. Any excuse to cuddle a kitten." Holly patted the floor beside her. Buster took the hint and curled up next to her, his muzzle resting on her thigh so he could keep an eye on his kitten. Holly took turns petting the two animals and simply enjoying their presence. She started when Jeremy spoke.

"The three of you make quite the picture. Do you mind?" He held up his cell phone questioningly.

"Go ahead." Holly flushed with pleasure. "But, only if you join us for a selfie next."

"Deal." Jeremy snapped a couple of photos, then joined the crew on the floor in front of the fireplace, shifting Buster to his lap and slipping his arm around Holly's shoulder. His attempts to get all of them in the frame of the photo had Holly giggling.

She finally took the phone from him and snapped several photos before handing it back.

Jeremy held the phone out where she could see it and flipped through the photos. "Those are great. I'll send them to you in a bit. Are you still planning to leave?"

"Yes, but I've had a wonderful time." She scooped Angel into her hand and pushed herself to her feet. When Jeremy joined her, she handed him the sleeping kitten. "Take good care of her. Be sure to send me a picture after her bath. I'm interested in seeing the results."

"I will." Jeremy took Angel and tucked her into the crook of his arm before wrapping his free arm around Holly and drawing her close. She melted against him, lifting her face for a kiss which he gladly bestowed. When the kiss ended, he grinned at her. "So, can I see you again sometime soon?"

"Are you kidding? You're a great guy and you love animals as much as I do." Holly flashed him a wicked grin. "Will you marry me?"

"Now *that's* an interesting proposition." Jeremy tightened his grip, drawing Holly even closer. "But, I must warn you—I have a strict three-date rule before marriage can be discussed."

"Three dates you say?" Holly cocked her head and batted her eyes at Jeremy in her best femme fatale impression. "So, when did you say you wanted to see me again?"

About the Author

Isabella Norse scored major "cool mom" points by playing the same video games as her sons and their friends. In these virtual worlds she slayed demons and destroyed machines bent on galactic extermination while simultaneously wooing cocky assassins and sexy aliens. She fell in love with the make-believe worlds and rich characters that inhabited them and now writes her own tales of love, romance, and adventure.

Still a gamer – and still cool – Isabella lives in Georgia with her husband and a herd of rescue cats. She loves to hear from readers and can be found on Facebook[1], Twitter[2], Pinterest[3], and Goodreads[4].

Social Media:

Sign up for my newsletter here: http://madmimi.com/signups/112968/join

Amazon Author Page: http://amazon.com/author/isabellanorse

Website: http://www.isabellanorse.com/

---

1.   https://www.facebook.com/IsabellaNorseAuthor

2.   https://twitter.com/AuthorIzzy

3.   https://www.pinterest.com/isabellanorse/

4.   https://www.goodreads.com/IsabellaNorse

Facebook: https://www.facebook.com/IsabellaNorseAuthor/

Twitter: https://twitter.com/AuthorIzzy

Pinterest: https://www.pinterest.com/isabellanorse/

"A Rescue Before Christmas"

By Amy Craig

Kate opened the front door of the renovated mid-century home and set down her laptop bag. It slumped over on the polished black concrete floor. She felt like joining it, but two brown and white wirehaired fox terriers barked a cheerful greeting from their high-end dog crates.

Puck yapped and bowed as she slipped off her heels and walked toward him. She stuck her hand through the grate of the crate door and scratched his snout. "Who's your favorite dog sitter? Yes, it's me. Did you miss me, little man?"

The feisty dog pawed the gate and barked in excitement. His brother turned in circles and tried to make his barks heard over the cacophony coming from Puck.

"I know, Gatsby. I didn't forget you, champ." She opened their crates and divided her attention between the playful animals. "Let's get the both of you fed."

After tummy rubs and good-natured nibbles, she saw Puck eyeing a vintage tinsel Christmas tree and redirected him toward his owner's manicured yard. "I don't think so, buddy. It's a balmy sixty degrees. You do your business outside."

She opened the sliding glass doors and the incorrigible dogs made a beeline for the manicured yard. They ran in joyful circles and checked their holes and hiding spots before relieving themselves on a carpet of bright green ryegrass.

Kate dished out two servings of raw food and placed the meat into monogrammed bowls. She set the bowls on the covered patio and returned to the main kitchen. She opened the built-in refrigerator and asked, "What am I going to eat?"

The appliance held a mixture of cured cheeses, antipasto, and chilled wines. She grabbed some olives and said, "Lovely. Harry and his partner are ready for a cocktail party."

The mobile dog groomer pulled into the driveway and announced her arrival with a cheerful honk. Kate waited for Holly to hook up her electrical connection and come inside. When the woman let herself into the house, Kate smiled at the groomer's combination of sensible scrubs, short blonde hair, and screaming pink tennis shoes.

"Hey, Holly. I like your haircut."

"Thanks! I just got tired of throwing it up in a pony."

"I've been thinking about cutting mine too."

"No!" Holly said, her face paling as she looked at Kate's curls. "I would kill for your hair."

Kate tucked the tumultuous mess behind her ears. "They're just a lot to manage."

The groomer nodded her head. "I hear ya. Are the dogs ready?"

"Yep, but Harry left a note. Puck just had an abscess removed from his ear and he wants to make sure you know about it so you don't inadvertently nick a swollen spot."

The groomer nodded and waved her phone. "Yep. He texted me too."

Kate smiled and the women silently acknowledged Harry and his partner's love for the two dogs. "I'm surprised they even went out of town. Those dogs are their babies."

Holly laughed. "Even dog parents need a break. I hear Miami is a lot of fun over the holidays."

They watched the dogs play chase in the yard before Holly said, "The ear doesn't seem to be bothering him, but I'll use scissors to make the edges neat."

Kate nodded her thanks, grateful Holly would spend the extra time to keep everyone out of trouble. She found Puck's lead and lured him to the house with a treat before handing the sweet boy over to the groomer. Gatsby padded toward the house, lonely and forlorn. "Don't worry, little man," she said as she leaned down to pet him, "I'm taking you to get my dinner."

She leashed the second terrier and loaded him into the passenger seat of her white sedan. When she rolled down the window, the playful dog stuck his nose out and tasted the wind. Kate shook her head as they arrived at the restaurant and the terrier pawed the door. "The car might be old and clunky, but the interiors are the least of my worries."

The dog nosed the bag and wagged his tail when she returned to the car with a grilled chicken salad. "Absolutely not," Kate said with an affectionate laugh. "You're an easy side gig and I need to pay off my student loans."

The winter sun had set by the time they returned to the flat-roofed house. Holly's van hummed in the driveway as Kate poured herself a glass of wine, ate her salad, and used her laptop to review legal precedents for her job. When the groomer came inside to swap dogs, Kate scratched Puck's head and snapped a picture for Harry when the happy dog seemed to smile. "Yes, you're very handsome!"

"Alexa, play Christmas music."

Kate wrinkled her nose as a remix of Jimmy Boyd's "I Saw Mommy Kissing Santa Claus" filled the house. "I guess I should have been more specific. Alexa, play 'Winter Wonderland' by Louis Armstrong."

The musician's gravelly voice made Kate smile. The slow tempo soothed her as she sipped her wine. "This is as close as I'm getting to snow in Louisiana."

An hour later, Gatsby bounded into the room and greeted his brother. Holly followed with an empty lead, but the generally cheerful groomer seemed troubled. She glanced over her shoulder and said, "There's a clumsy white dog sitting at the end of the driveway."

"Clumsy?"

"Long legs and big chestnut-colored paws. It doesn't look full grown."

The two women returned to the front door and looked toward the street. Beyond the ornamental trees and landscape lighting, a forlorn dog sat at the end of the drive. When a car drove past, it shied away from the noise and settled on the chilled asphalt. The dog rested its square head to its paws and waited.

"It's lean. Do you recognize it?"

Kate shook her head. "Maybe it belongs to a neighbor?"

Holly shook her head. "Doubtful. There's no collar."

Kate whistled and the dog looked up. After a moment of hesitation, it padded toward the house and stopped short. She checked the dog's gender and said, "Come here, sweet girl."

The dog licked its lips but stayed put.

"She's probably hungry."

Kate glanced at the home's polished black floors. "I can't bring her inside. Harry's kind of particular about the house."

"I can probably catch her and take her to the pound. Or you can call animal control."

"I guess you encounter a lot of strays."

The groomer nodded. "She could have gotten loose. Animal control will hold her in case someone claims her."

Kate thought of the numerous construction sites lining the street. The large lots were prime for redevelopment and she had pulled the terriers away from trash and scraps the last time she housesat. "I doubt it."

She reentered the house, closed the sliding glass doors, and pulled a hunk of cheese from the refrigerator. Holly began disconnecting her truck as Kate returned to the driveway and faced the stray dog.

"Come here, girl. I hope you're not a howler." She offered the animal a sniff of cheese and led her toward the safety of the manicured yard. When they got to the side gate, she tossed the cheese in the yard. The dog considered her options and loped toward the offering.

Kate laughed. "You're a cheap date."

After the dog gobbled up the expensive morsel, Kate extended her hand and let the animal examine it. She stroked the dog's face and smiled. "At least you've got good taste."

The terriers barking and dancing on the other side of the glass had a different opinion. "Absolutely not," Kate said as she shook her head. Mindful of her obligations, she closed the side gate and left the stray in the yard. Holly waved before she got in her truck and drove off, leaving Kate with three animals and a mountain of work.

She dished up an extra helping of dog food and placed the bowl on the covered patio along with a full container of water. The white dog walked over and sniffed the food, then circled and settled down on the concrete.

Puck and Gatsby sprinted back and forth along the glass, hoping the barrier would dissolve and allow them enough freedom to explore their guest. The white dog waited, her large head resting on her paws. When the terriers finally lost interest in the strange dog, they sought out their beds and Kate closed her laptop with a sigh. "I might have to work through the holidays to meet my billing quota."

The terriers ignored her and she took them for a quick walk before she readied them for bed. The household seemed to be at peace, but a deep bark echoed through the polished rooms. Both terriers looked up and tested their vocal cords as they replied to the white dog's alarm. "Shh," Kate said as she led them back to their beds and rubbed their backs. The dogs submitted to the attention, but their ears remained perked, waiting for the white dog to sound the alarm. After several minutes, they settled at the foot of the guest bed where Kate would sleep and she permitted herself to take a deep breath.

Unable to settle down, she went outside and considered the white dog, stark against the illuminated concrete and black night sky. The animal's lean sides swelled and sank as it breathed and watched her, uncertain of its place and the neighborhood's unfamiliar sounds. Kate sat down and ran a hand along the animal's flank. The dog thumped its tail and lifted its head, curious and constrained.

"You're a sweet girl, aren't you?" She lifted the dog's paw, tipped with chestnut brown. "You're going to be huge, aren't you? Ninety pounds?"

The dog yawned and settled its head on her lap.

She pulled out her phone. "Let's get some pictures and post them on social media. Maybe someone will recognize you."

The dog closed its eyes.

"Maybe not."

KATE WOKE UP IN THE guest room when the terriers began to stir with the sun. She checked social media and sighed. "Not a single response. I guess everyone was sleeping."

She led a yipping parade toward the kitchen and smiled when she saw the white dog asleep against the window. Water dampened the concrete and kibble surrounded an empty food bowl. "We'll give them a day or so to come find you."

A morning walk with the terriers brightened her spirits. She fixed a cup of coffee and hoped her energy levels would carry her through her commute and a morning of case files. She fed all the animals and commended Puck and Gatsby when they retreated to their crates. "It won't be a late night, boys."

Her supervisor had a different game plan for the day. Andrew printed out a copy of her case law comments and returned them to her with red ink. "You're getting too tied up in the backstory. Focus on the decisions and the facts."

"They're not mutually exclusive."

"Don't make life harder on yourself, Kate. I'm trying to teach you best practices to help you succeed at this firm."

"Harry said it's important to pay attention to the subtleties."

"Harry started the firm. He can say whatever he wants to say. Nobody is going to fire him."

Kate nodded and focused on the screen of her laptop.

"You might have to stay late the rest of the week."

The threat brought a rush of adrenaline to her system. She dropped her tactful defense and said, "Tomorrow is the Holiday Hoopla."

"What the hell is that?"

"It's a fundraiser for the Family Law Society."

Andrew rolled his eyes. "Pick a pro-bono cause with better returns."

"Like personal injuries suits? Class action settlements? What do you suggest?"

Andrew shook his head and wandered off to find someone else to harass.

At the end of the day, she picked up Greek takeout and returned to the mid-century house. She checked her social media accounts for leads, but the internet was silent. She sighed and settled in a wire chair on the patio. The white dog sniffed her meal and sat, as composed as a marble statue, while the terriers barked from their crates.

Kate withdrew a piece of meat and offered it to the stray. "I can't keep you here, pretty girl. It's not my house and I share an apartment with three other lawyers. You need room to run."

The dog dropped her belly to the ground and barked.

"I'm going to feed the princes and let them loose. Do you promise not to eat them?"

The dog rolled over and wagged her tail.

"Excellent strategy. They're a little high strung, but they mean well."

Kate stood by, prepared to intervene as Puck and Gatsby charged the big white dog. The terriers barked and darted while the stray rolled to her side and stared up at Kate with the patience of a saint. "Okay, pups, we've established who's in charge. Go run!"

The three dogs rolled and played until Kate delivered their meals to the patio. Even though the white dog's impromptu plastic dish loomed over the terriers' monogrammed bowls, all three dogs ate their meals with enthusiastic delicacy.

Someone knocked on the door and Kate entered the house and found a neighbor eager to peer inside Harry's home. Her sandy blond hair almost hid the streaks of gray, but her walking attire looked like it had remained consistent since the nineties. She ignored Kate's greeting and said, "I keep thinking I hear a big dog in the backyard."

Kate smiled and tried to block the older woman from entering the house.

"I don't think so, Mrs. Barbara."

"Are you quite sure? No one on this street has a big dog. I walk twice a day. I would know. I should probably call Harry."

"I wouldn't want to ruin their vacation."

"Are you sure you haven't seen a large dog?"

"What color?"

"Excuse me?"

"I would keep an eye out for missing animal posters. Maybe you could check telephone poles and the bulletin board by the elementary school? If you see a dog that matches a description, the best thing to do might be to call the phone number on that sign."

"Oh, that's a good idea."

Kate eased the door closed. "Have a nice walk, Mrs. Barbara."

She brought her laptop outside and offered all three dogs a rawhide treat. They chewed in silence while she finished her takeout and considered her caseload. The symphony of night bugs swelled as the three dogs sprawled in a pile of easy snores and Kate pecked at the keyboard. When she was sure the neighborhood slept, she escorted the terriers inside, rubbed the white dog's nose, and wished her companions a quiet goodnight.

HEAVY CLOUDS HUNG OVER the city the next morning. Kate led the white dog outside and considered her sedan. "You might fit."

The animal eyed the vehicle and pulled against the lead.

"C'mon, girl. The shelter won't be that bad."

She dropped her belly to the ground and whined. Her pink nose twitched and she inched back toward the house.

Kate unhooked the lead. She tugged the stray's borrowed collar, hoping the gentle suggestion would incentivize the animal to accept the car. When nothing happened, she withdrew a piece of jerky from her pocket and tossed it on the seat.

The dog sniffed the offering.

"Okay, you can have two."

The dog sat and barked.

Kate winced and scanned the street for Mrs. Barbara. She eyed the animal and decided on surprise and brute force. The animal's tender pink skin tickled her nose as she lifted it and staggered toward the backseat. "At least I was smart enough not to wear black."

Morning traffic on Interstate 10 slowed their progress toward north Baton Rouge. Kate kept an eye on the sedan's temperature sensor and watched it climb beneath the shadows of raindrops. "We're almost there," she said to reassure herself. "Traffic's usually not this bad."

A flashing red light bloomed on the console ten minutes before the car died. Kate swore and engaged her hazards as she drifted toward the shoulder. "The mechanic warned me this might happen."

The dog kept its head down and eyed the parade of cars zooming past them.

"It's okay. I have roadside assistance."

Forty-five minutes later, Kate's empty coffee cup mocked her and she had a series of voicemails from Andrew questioning her whereabouts. "Maybe he'll order me a new laptop for Christmas," she said before she listened to his third message.

When his next voicemail defined at-will employment, she tapped her fingers on the steering wheel and sighed. "Maybe not."

She smiled in relief when a huge red tow truck slowed alongside her vehicle and parked in front of her sedan. The truck's yellow flashing lights shone through the morning rainstorm, and the white dog tried to jump the center console and claim the comfort of the passenger seat. Kate blocked her progress and said, "I don't think so!"

The man that climbed down from the cab wore a yellow fluorescent safety vest, a helmet, and a pair of leather gloves. Kate expected a grizzled old operator, but the driver was close to thirty and seemed ambivalent about the rain. Kate tried not to ogle him as she rolled down her window and smiled.

He approached the sedan and flashed some form of identification.

She ignored the credentials and examined the tattoos swirling around his biceps. They disappeared beneath the cut-off sleeves of his coveralls. She raised her gaze and met his ice-blue eyes.

He glanced at the dog and asked, "Are you Kate Smith?"

Kate cleared her throat. "I am."

"Troy Stewart." He handed her a clipboard and asked her to sign for the services. "Can you call someone to come get the dog?"

"Um, if I could call someone, I wouldn't have called you."

"No family?"

"I don't think that's relevant."

The driver raised an eyebrow and eyed his truck. "Fine. Your dog can ride in the cab."

"She's actually not my dog. I'm bringing her to animal control."

An airplane flew over the interstate and overpowered his reply.

"Excuse me?"

"I said we could stop at the pound."

Kate glanced at the dog in the side mirror. Wet nose pressed against the glass, the animal looked more interested in licking the tow driver than defending Kate's domain. "Really?" she asked as the animal took advantage of her disbelief and claimed the front seat.

"Sure. It doesn't seem like you have a lot of options right now."

Kate reached for the leash and hooked the stray without admonishing her. "That's really considerate. I mean. I wasn't sure what I was going to do with her when you showed up."

"You can't leave her on the interstate."

"I would never do that!"

"Good. Get out on the passenger side if you can."

Kate scrambled past the dog, grabbed her purse, and eased open the passenger side door. The driver held the leash while she climbed into the cab of the red tow truck. She had expected stale cigarettes and engine oil, but the interior was remarkably clean.

When she looked down, the driver and the dog were having a standoff. Raindrops diluted the puddle of yellow pee spreading from the man's leather work boots. He eyed the animal with suspicion and seemed willing to reconsider his proposition.

"I am so sorry!" Kate said. "We've been stuck in the car for an hour. She's really a sweet dog."

"Will she bite me if I pick her up?"

"I don't think so. That's how I got her in the sedan. I told you she's not my dog."

The dog looked at her like she was a traitor, but consented when the driver lifted her toward the cab.

Kate opened her arms and received the dog. She wrapped an arm around the animal and whispered, "That was unnecessary! He's being super helpful."

The animal cocked its head and licked Kate. She felt the whisper of its whiskers and wiped away the beads of moisture left by the rain.

The driver monitored the interstate traffic as he loaded her disabled sedan. She watched him center the vehicle on the bed, tie it down with straps, and chock and block the wheels. "I think we're in good hands," she said to the dog.

When the driver finished the task, he returned to the tow truck and removed his helmet.

"This is a really impressive truck," Kate said as a peace offering.

The driver eyed the dog and finished his paperwork.

"How much can it tow?"

"Gross vehicle weight 26,000 pounds. The rest is lagniappe; 22' steel rollback body with aluminum side rails, 10K winch, two toolboxes, and polished doors." He put the vehicle in gear and added, "Dog fur wasn't an option."

Kate kept quiet while he merged with traffic. "Take this first exit."

She used her phone to guide him through the series of low buildings and anonymous streets surrounding the airport. Thick trees surrounded the animal shelter, but Kate pointed out the entrance.

The driver slowed on the gravel as a sign directed them to the back of the facility. When he cut the powerful engine, a cacophony of barks filled the silence. The white dog whimpered.

"It won't be that bad," Kate said.

The driver raised an eyebrow.

"I'll be fast."

He climbed down and helped her lift the dog from the cab. Kate leashed it and pulled, but the dog sat in the rain and refused to budge.

Kate eyed the chain-link exterior pens and haphazard outbuildings surrounding the facility. Men in blue shirts loitered on a loading dock and admired the tow truck while they smoked.

"C'mon, girl," Kate said. "Your family will find you. You just have to wait it out."

The dog took a few hesitant steps, sniffed the air, and bolted to the tow truck.

Kate found herself holding an empty lead. She looked at the driver and told herself not to cry. "I swear I'm not trying to surrender my dog. I just want to keep her off the streets."

"I know it's not your dog."

"Troy, I kind of need some help."

The driver nodded and extended his hand. Kate gave him the lead and watched him approach the dog. The animal whimpered and eyed the building. He murmured reassurances to her and hooked the lead.

"Do you want me to carry her in?"

"No. I'll bring her."

Five minutes later, they were back where they had started.

Troy checked his phone. "My aunt volunteers at a shelter in Gonzales. It's possible they would take her."

Kate shook her head. "I spent all night researching rescue organizations and foster groups. They won't accept dogs from different parishes. Or they won't accept dogs without temperament tests. Or you have to pay for full veterinary support." She eyed the drab shelter and said, "I just can't take responsibility for her."

"They're decent people, Kate. Companion Animal Alliance is building a new shelter down by the university."

"But this is where I have to leave her. Look at her. She's scared. What if she has already been here?"

The dog eyed both of them and howled.

The shelter inhabitants listened for a moment and returned her mournful cry.

TROY USED HIS FOREARM to wipe the rain from his face. He turned on the heat and said, "It's eleven o'clock."

Kate pulled some tissues from her purse and did her best to clean up her mascara. "I can pay you for your time."

Troy laughed and said, "I don't want your money. I've been up since 5 AM. I want lunch."

"Like a drive-thru?"

"Not enough clearance."

"I could wait in the car while you grab something."

"The rain's about to stop." He considered her sleeveless dress and said, "You probably need to go to work."

Kate nodded, "Yeah, but I could eat."

The wet dog rubbed her head against the roof of the car. Kate tried to brush away the residue of white fur, but it drifted down to the seat. "You don't have to do this."

"Most people would have dragged the dog inside or asked the employees to come get her." He checked the mirrors and put the truck in gear.

"She looked miserable."

"She did."

The dog thumped her tail.

"She's going to get bigger," he said. "What is she? Some kind of cross between a Great Dane and a Pit Bull?"

"I dunno. 'Lab' sounds more approachable."

Troy eyed the dog.

"I just can't keep her."

"You said that."

He drove toward the levee and stopped at a cluster of painted cinder block buildings posing as a po'boy restaurant. Glittered poinsettias crowded the grimy windows, but a line of people stretched out the door.

Kate eyed the distant tower where she should be at work. "At least let me buy lunch."

Troy grinned. "I'm not going to stop you."

They ordered two sandwiches, iced teas, and a bag of fries.

When they returned to the truck, the dog sniffed their haul and waited, too scared to jump. Troy lifted her down and Kate clipped her lead onto the dog's collar.

They carried their feast across River Road and climbed the side of the levee. Wet grass stuck to Kate's shoes and coated her legs. She used a wad of napkins to dry the black metal bench waiting at the top of the levee. Troy ignored the moisture and plopped down on the bench.

"Don't you have other calls to take?"

He took a bite of his fully dressed oyster po'boy and popped an errant pickle in his mouth. "Independent operator."

"What does that mean?"

"It means I don't respond to accident scenes or participate in a police rotation system. I don't conduct private property tows. Don't do parking tickets or repossessions. I cherry-pick my calls and avoid the sob stories and shenanigans.

"You'll have to add 'damsel in distress with opinionated dog' to your list of screen outs."

"I don't know. It's working out so far." He took another bite of his sandwich and said, "Why don't you let her off the lead?"

"She might run."

"Problem solved."

"That's not very responsible."

"Ha. That's my theme for the day."

Kate took a bite of her sandwich and ran her hand along the dog's ribs. She pulled an oyster from her po'boy and offered it to the dog, who lifted it from her fingers with a nuzzle of hot breath.

"What about you, Ms. Smith? What's your gig?"

"Real estate, probate and trust law."

"That sounds awful."

"It is. For now." She took a sip of her tea. "Who thinks you're irresponsible?"

"My brother."

Kate eyed his tattoos and picked out the symbols she recognized.

"We played football together. We joined the Marines together. We thought it would be a dream to open a garage together."

"It's not working out?"

"He got married and reevaluated his priorities. Now he wants quantity over quality. I told him that wasn't his call."

Kate finished her tea and asked, "What are you going to do?"

He leaned back on his elbows and said, "Dissolve the partnership."

"Ouch."

"Pretty much."

His cell phone rang and he answered the call, "Hello?"

Kate tried to give him some privacy. She glanced down the levee and considered her sedan sitting on the back of the tow truck. She wondered whether to send it to the driver's repair shop or find a reputable dealership to take care of the problem. Then she recalled the last repair quote she had gotten and realized she had more than one reason to return to work.

"I'll be back in an hour or so," Troy said before he hung up the phone. He finished his sandwich and asked, "So what are you going to do with the dog?"

Kate blew out her breath and scratched the dog's ears. "Find someone to take her."

"Why can't you keep her?"

"I live in an apartment and work all day. She needs room to run."

"We all do."

Kate nodded. "Yeah, but I slaved through three years of law school to get this job. Catered lunches buffer the twelve-hour days, but she didn't sign up for that life."

Troy stared at the muddy Mississippi running beneath the light gray skies. Tugs fought the current and pulled barges stacked with red and white containers beneath the bridge. "Sometimes it's better to renegotiate your deal."

"I don't have that kind of leverage."

Her phone rang and she prayed it was not Andrew. She considered the local area code and said, "This is Kate Smith."

The voice on the other end of the line chattered for a few minutes. The dog emitted a low growl, lifted her chestnut tinged paw, and settled it in Kate's lap. Kate nodded and asked the caller, "Can you describe any special features? She's mostly white, but she has a few special markings."

She toyed with the animal's soft fur while she listened to the caller's obfuscations. "Just to be sure, could you send me a picture?"

The caller hung up and Kate shook her head. "You were right, girl, he was up to no good."

The dog dropped her paw and settled at Kate's feet.

"I'm taking this is a sign. Have you considered completely overhauling your life to accommodate a pet?"

Kate squinted in the midday sunlight and stared at the man.

"Right, that's just me."

Troy draped his arm along the back of the bench and said, "Most people would have taken one look at that dopey mutt, barred the gate, and called animal control."

Kate felt the warmth of his body against the cool December air. "I'm not most people."

"True. Most people wouldn't be sitting on this levee."

The wind off the river blew a curl in front of her face. She tucked it behind her ear and said, "I should probably get back to work."

He toyed with the ends of her hair and said, "Or not."

Kate smiled and turned to face him. His eyes shone against the gray winter sky and the muted colors of the levee. She leaned toward him and said, "I guess I could call it a mental health day."

Troy nodded and focused on her lips. Kate bit the inside of her cheek and moved to meet him halfway as a bicyclist whizzed past them. The dog raised its head and gave chase before either of them could react. As they scrambled upright, their forgotten lunches and icy drinks tumbled to the pavement.

Kate ran after the dog and called, "Come on, girl. Please come back!" She struggled in her heels as the bicyclist glanced over his shoulder, considered the parade of misfits, and increased his speed.

The dog slowed as Troy lunged for her lead. "Nice try, mutt."

Kate dropped her hands to her knees and huffed. "This is getting ridiculous."

Troy strolled up and presented the leash. Kate laughed at the stray, whose tongue lolled from her mouth.

"So that's your flavor."

Troy ran a hand through his hair. "As much as I've enjoyed the morning, I should probably get your car to a repair shop and go sort things out with my brother."

Kate took a deep breath. "Yeah. I guess we'll have to take this sweet girl back to the shelter."

"Why don't I keep her for a few nights? That will give you a little time to contact rescue groups and decide what you want to do."

"Why would you do that?"

"It'll guarantee me a second date."

Kate blushed. "You already have my car."

"You might choose another repair shop."

"Well, who's fixing my car? You or your brother?"

The driver laughed. "He stays in the business office. I'll have one of the mechanics do it."

"The cooling system keeps overheating."

Troy glanced at the sedan. "Most overheating problems in a sealed system can be traced to gasket failure, leaks or worn components."

Kate thought of the odometer and the series of cross-country road trips she had taken to relocate for her summer internships. "I'd put my money on worn components."

Troy put his hands in his pockets. "Skip the gambling, Kate. You've got enough debts."

He drove them downtown and used the truck to stop traffic in front of her office building. "How are you getting home?"

"I'll call a rideshare."

He nodded. "Come to the garage tomorrow after you get off work. I'll call you if it's going to take longer."

"What are you going to feed her?"

He glanced at the dog wedged between them. "We'll manage."

Kate nodded and tried not to feel lonely as she faced the gleaming glass tower that would never feel like a home. She considered Troy's sleeveless attire and wondered if his closet contained more of the same attire. "There's a party tonight..."

He shook his head. "I don't do fancy."

She smiled. "How do you know it's going to be fancy?"

"Call it a hunch."

"It's a fundraiser."

"Definitely fancy."

"The City Club is rolling out the red carpet."

"You have fun, then."

"Are you sure? They make really good food. And there's an open bar. Worst case scenario, you'll go home well fed."

"Best case scenario?"

"We dance."

"I said 'best case scenario.'"

Kate laughed. "I can meet you there."

"You don't want to show up in a tow truck?"

Kate tucked a strand of hair behind her ear. "It's not that. I have to be there early to help set-up the silent auction."

He smiled. "This party sounds like a dud."

"Six o'clock?"

He eyed her dress and said, "I hope you have another outfit."

"I do. I think you'll like it."

"I'm counting on it."

A car honked and he raised his hand to acknowledge the suggestion. She gave him the details one more time and climbed down from the truck. As he pulled away, she stood on the sidewalk and brushed the grass and dog hair from her dress.

AFTER A FEW HOURS OF unproductivity, she realized the chaos of the morning was more interesting than disciplined work. She kept thinking about the dog and the man with the ice-blue eyes sitting on the levee. What would have happened next if they had let the remainder of the day unfold with only the pleasure of two carefree beating hearts to govern them?

She called an early ride and returned to the mid-century home. A robotic vacuum whirled over the polished black floors while the terriers bounced in their crates. She greeted the dogs and released them to chase the robot. They ran in circles and came back to her, sniffing her dress for signs of their clumsy new friend.

"She's going to be okay," Kate promised.

A sleek red dress waited for her in the guest room closet. The flared skirt and sleeveless top teased the line between secretary and seductress. She caressed the thrift store fabric and acknowledged having an audience would make the dress more fun to wear.

The City Club boasted brass chandeliers and coffered ceilings, but none of the evening's fundraising participants cared about floor-to-ceiling windows or dark mahogany woodwork.

A big band played standards from the 1950s while tuxedo-clad waiters circulated with trays of martinis on vintage serving trays.

"Welcome to the Holiday Hoopla!" Kate said as she checked in a new group of people. She showed them how to bid on their smartphones. An older woman tapped her feet in time with the music and grabbed back her phone. "I know how to use it!"

Kate smiled and turned to greet the next guest.

Troy toyed with a rotary phone and a stack of LIFE magazines meant to offset the wait. His white dress shirt and dark gray blazer camouflaged his profession, but Kate would have recognized him anywhere.

"Do you know how to use it?" she asked. He looked up and she caught the flash of appreciation as he scanned her dress.

"You look good, Kate Smith. The eyeliner was a nice touch."

She smiled and handed him a brochure. "You look pretty good yourself."

"How long do you have to work?"

"Not too much longer on my shift. The committee members will start their comedy sketches when the band takes a break."

A look of panic flashed across his face.

"The climax is a send-up from Santa's Elves and a light-up bar cart."

He glanced toward the exit staircase and she laughed. "Don't worry, I'm almost done. Keep an eye out for the stuffed mushrooms and smoked salmon canapés. They're delicious."

It took longer than she expected to finish checking people in for the event. When she closed the table, she worried she would find Troy standing in a corner, but she found him holding court with a city councilman and an orthopedic surgeon.

"Drivers don't move over when they see the flashing lights. They slow down, scan the scene, and see if it's worth their attention."

The surgeon nodded and took a sip of his drink. "That's when the mistakes happen. Senseless vehicle collisions are funding my practice. An ounce of common sense could save this state millions of dollars."

"Publicity isn't the problem. Drivers know about the 'Move Over Law.'"

Troy eyed the councilman's Tabasco Brand tie. "That doesn't mean they follow it. Especially with tow trucks. Until people start hearing about enforcement and citations, they're only going to move over when it's convenient."

Kate put her hand on Troy's left arm and he smiled before shaking hands with his new acquaintances. He made a show of leaning back and examining her outfit. "That's a good look for you."

"I thought you would like it."

"A little retro..."

She raised her hand and waved toward the starburst decorations and the sounds of the band. "We decided to roll with it."

The band started a slow song and she said, "Dance with me?"

He nodded and pulled her close. "So we're raising money for Family Law?"

She nodded and tried to enjoy the heat of his body. The sweet smell of bourbon on his breath merged with his cologne in a tantalizing combination.

"What kind of Family Law?"

"Foster Care. Post-Emancipation Services."

"Is this a personal cause?"

She nodded and refused to look at him.

"How personal?"

She met his gaze and said, "I grew up in foster care."

He nodded and continued to lead her around the floor. She waited for his pity and prejudiced questions, but he remained silent until the song ended. They stood face to face as he said, "You've done a lot to be proud of."

She thought of Andrew's spiteful critiques and the hours she had spent working toward the firm's financial goals. "I don't know, I feel like I got a little lost along the way. My professors kept reinforcing my success and I followed their suggestions without thinking about what I wanted to do the most."

A group of men and women in elf costumes began to assemble near the band. Troy pulled Kate toward the patio where a few intrepid souls smoked cigarettes in the evening air. They took one look at Troy and Kate before stubbing out their cigarettes.

Troy removed his jacket and handed it to her. She slipped into the warmth and felt the smooth lining settle over her shoulders. "When you said you didn't have family, I just figured you were just from out of town."

Kate looked at him and said, "I am."

"How far?"

"Illinois."

"Well, at least you got an upgrade."

She smiled and crossed her arms. "Are you really going to dissolve the partnership with your brother?"

He caressed her cheek. "You think I should give him another chance?"

She nodded.

"Well, he is looking after your dog for me."

"Is she doing okay?"

He pulled her close. "Mm-hmm."

"Do you think she missed me this afternoon?"

He lowered his head. "Not as much as I did."

His lips felt firm and hot against hers as the cool wind blowing off the Mississippi River surrounded them. Kate leaned into the kiss, cocooned by his arms and the satin binding of his sport coat.

"You've got a big heart, Kate Smith. One day you'll tell me how you earned it."

She smiled and slipped off his jacket. "But tonight?"

He accepted the jacket and said, "I'm on call at 5 AM."

"I'm really glad you came to the fundraiser, Troy."

He glanced at the costumed crowd and the middle-aged lawyers ending their comedy routine. "It's not my usual crowd."

THE NEIGHBORHOOD'S quiet streets and subdued landscape lighting welcomed Kate before she pulled into Harry's driveway and let herself into the house. Instead of pulling out her laptop or pouring a glass of wine, she slipped off her heels and walked along the gallery walls, wondering how many billable hours it took to support a collection of fine art.

She stopped in front of her favorite painting. A flock of Technicolor parakeets surrounded a portrait of the two terriers in Panama hats. The eccentric black signature in the corner proved Harry and his partner had not only envisioned the artwork, but had also shelled out enough money to convince someone with an ego to paint it.

She picked up her cell phone and dialed Harry's personal number.

"Are the doggies okay?"

Kate glanced at the animals digging holes beneath the jasmine trellis. "Sure, they're fine."

"And the house?"

She scanned the curated Christmas decorations presiding over supple leather couches and polished surfaces. "Perfectly intact."

Harry sighed. "We're about to do to go for a nightcap. What do you need, darlin'?"

Kate smiled at the endearment and the gentle reminder that Harry and his partner had trusted her enough to set aside their worries and go on vacation. He had served as her mentor and had often counseled her over happy hour specials when she needed advice about managing her colleagues or approaching a certain judge. Despite the hour, she took a deep breath and said, "I changed my mind about the judicial clerkship for Family Court. Will you still write me a recommendation? It's a tight deadline."

Harry laughed. "I told you trust law was lucrative but boring."

She smiled and flopped on the guest bed. "Yeah. You were right."

"Send me the paperwork and I'll finish it before we come home."

"One other thing," she said.

"What is it?"

"Andrew is kind of an ass."

Harry laughed and relayed the comment to his partner. "He's just bitter. He knows he'll never make partner."

"I might not make partner either."

"That's okay, dear. Your career is going to last forty years. The key is to make sure it hardly feels like work."

Kate hung up the phone and spent an hour tossing balls for Puck and Gatsby. She made a list of names for the white dog and wondered how Troy and the sweet girl were getting along. She thought of calling Troy and realized she had given him the dog, but she did not have his number. She pulled the towing paperwork from her purse and wondered which brother would answer if she called late at night.

The next morning, she walked the terriers, called a car to get to work, and smiled pleasantly when Andrew assigned her to a slew of extra cases. She tried not to check her phone as the hours passed, but at five o'clock, she logged out of her computer and packed her bag.

"Where are you going?"

"To pick up my car."

"Have it delivered. Your little accident put us behind on depositions."

"It wasn't an accident, Andrew. And no, I'm not staying late. You can have my fortune cookie."

She sorted her email as her driver fought Baton Rouge traffic.

"When are they going to build a loop?" she asked out loud.

The driver smiled and glanced in the rearview mirror. "You new in town?"

Kate nodded. "A little less than a year."

"It's gonna take you a might longer to figure out dis town." He shook his head and whistled as a woman ignored the safety of a crosswalk and began weaving through traffic. "People here been managing their troubles for so long they forgot what it's like to learn."

"Old dogs and new tricks?"

The man laughed and slapped the steering wheel. "Somethin' like that!"

WHEN THE DRIVER PULLED up at the mid-city garage, Kate identified the shiny red tow truck and Troy's muscled arms. He stood with his back to her, propping up the hood of an ancient vehicle while he counseled a client on what had gone wrong under the hood. A slow warmth spread through Kate's system and she smiled before she scanned the property for her car and her dog.

They both sat in the final bay, clean as a whistle and waiting for her.

"She needs a name," Troy said by way of greeting. "People keep asking about her. It's embarrassing to just call her 'dog'."

Kate rubbed the pup's head and asked, "Does someone want to adopt her?"

"A few people might have left their numbers. She seems happy enough to see you."

Kate crouched and rubbed the ridges above the dog's eyes. "I missed you too, mutt." She stood and scanned the busy garage. Christmas lights hung in the window between the waiting room and the service bays where mechanics diagnosed error codes and tightened bolts. She examined the crew and smiled when she realized their coveralls still had sleeves. She turned to Troy and asked, "Can you keep her for a while?"

He scratched his cheek and said, "Sure, but what will you call her?"

"Blanco? Coconut?"

Troy shook his head and questioned his life choices.

"Mooney? Dove?"

The dog groaned and put her chestnut paw on top of her head.

"How about something a little more authentic?"

Kate thought of their lunch on top of the levee. "What about 'Pearl'?"

The dog woofed and Troy leaned in for a kiss. The warmth of his lips revved her system, but someone whistled and laid on the horn.

Kate smiled as he pulled back and whispered, "Good choice. Let's go get your keys and settle your bill."

Pearl head-butted Kate and she scratched the dog's ears as she tested Troy's limits. "I hope you're giving me a discount."

Troy shook his head. "I've done enough good deeds this week."

"Free legal advice?"

He laughed and tugged Kate's hair before stealing a quick kiss.

She smiled at the lighthearted rebuke. His lips felt as warm as the sun and the kiss left behind a trace of mint lip balm. She raised her hand and touched her lips, curious to feel the evidence of where they had been.

Troy watched her move and grinned. "We'll work it out."

THE END

ABOUT THE
AUTHOR

Amy Craig lives in Baton Rouge, Louisiana with her family and a small menagerie of pets. She writes women's fiction and contemporary romances with intelligent and empathetic heroines. She can't always vouch for the men. She has worked as an engineer, project manager, and incompetent waitress. In her spare time, she plays tennis and expands her husband's honey-do list.

Look for the full-length conclusion of "A Rescue Before Christmas" in 2020 and follow Amy on social media to stay up-to-date on her new work.

Amazon: https://www.amazon.com/author/amycraig

Website: https://www.amy-craig.com/

Twitter: https://twitter.com/authoramycraig

Facebook: https://www.facebook.com/AuthorAmy-Craig/

Goodreads: https://www.goodreads.com/author/show/18011214

BookBub: https://www.bookbub.com/authors/amy-craig

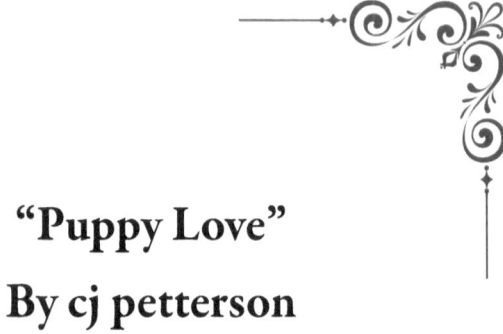

"Puppy Love"
By cj petterson

"**M**uffin, how in the world did you get up there?"

Standing on the top rung of the stepladder, Francesca DuBose gripped the edge of the roof with one hand, held her breath, and stretched as far as she could but still couldn't reach the kitten.

"C'mon over here, you little dickens."

None of her pleas, threats, or kitty treats enticed the tiny kitten to come close enough to where she could get a hand on it. She couldn't decide what frustrated her more, accidentally letting the calico kitten escape through the patio door or having to call the fire department to rescue the little daredevil.

"Oh, no," Francesca groaned when she heard a fire truck's siren wind down in front of her home. Certain that the commotion would attract a clot of curious neighbors, she ran to the front yard. She threw her hands up in frustration when she ran into her ex-boyfriend, Cody Phillips, as she rounded the corner of the house.

"Did you have to use the siren, Cody? I didn't say there was a fire," she said and pointed a finger at the bulky, turnout gear the firefighter was wearing. "I said I needed a pet rescue. My kitten escaped and got up on the roof, and I can't reach her."

The twinkle in his eyes betrayed his amusement, but he answered her complaint with a sober tone. "We have to use the siren on official runs, Frankie, and even something as non-emergent as a pet rescue is an official run. Now, where is your crisis?"

"Around back," Francesca said, as Cody and another firefighter followed her around to the patio. "Her name is Muffin because she was such a little ragamuffin when I got her."

"If it's only a kitten, I guess I don't need all this gear," Cody said and slipped out of his thick coat, laying it over one of the patio chairs.

"Another foster kitten?" he said as he stepped onto the bottom rung of the ladder that the other firefighter steadied.

Can't keep anything secret in a small town, she thought, *and Glen Eden, Alabama, definitely fits the bill there.* She hugged her sweater tighter against a gust of cool October wind. "I keep saying I'm not going to foster anymore, then the shelter calls me, and I can't say no."

He was up the ladder and back down with his fingers wrapped gently around the mewing kitten almost before she finished her sentence.

"Thank you," she said as she retrieved the wayward feline from Cody's hand.

"Thanks, Jonas," Cody said.

The other firefighter nodded at Francesca and left.

"I have no idea how she got up there," she said.

Cody pointed to a camellia bush with branches overhanging the eave. "Probably climbed that camellia on the corner.

You'll need to cut that back, or you'll have more than cats up there."

"I know, and the termite guy warned me it's also an avenue for ants and bugs to make their way into the attic and the rest of the house. But between working and fostering two cats and a special-needs puppy, I haven't had time to get my yard work done."

"Special needs?"

"Miss Molly was hit by a car and had to have a hind leg amputated." She immediately regretted her matter-of-fact statement when Cody winced. She knew she'd reminded him of those in his circle of friends who'd lost limbs while serving in the Armed Forces.

"I've had her for a few weeks now, and she's doing great with her rehab. Really she is. She's still in the kennel in the laundry room because I just got home from work, or she'd be all over this yard. She's supposed to be fitted for a prosthesis soon."

"They do that for dogs?"

"Wonderful, isn't it?"

"It's amazing." He hesitated after taking a step to leave. "By the way, if you'd like some help with your yard, I'm doing yard work for a few people on my off days."

Her foster care work hadn't been the only subject of town gossip lately. She'd heard he'd taken out a huge loan to pay off a mountain of debts his ex-wife ran up while he was off flying fighter jets in Afghanistan. *Those bills must've been doozies,* she thought. *He's been divorced for two years and out of the service for three, that's a long time to still be paying off someone else's debts.*

"I guess I could use help, but despite what people may think about lawyers' fees, I don't make—"

"I don't charge old girlfriends."

Ex-girlfriend, she thought, and the word "old" chafed her a bit also. "I appreciate the offer, Cody, but I'm already indebted to you for rescuing Muffin, and that's about more than I can afford."

"You don't owe me a thing. Rescuing cuties is part of my job."

She turned to survey the back yard. "I couldn't let you work for free. There are a lot of pine cones and deadfall on the ground, too."

"Might be two or three days' work for one man, but that's all."

Another scan of the unkempt backyard changed her mind. "Okay, but you have to give me a real bill for the time you're here. No special 'friend' deals."

Cody's smile crinkled the weathered corners of his hazel eyes. "Okay, no special deals."

She cuddled the purring Muffin close to her chest. "Thanks again for the rescue."

He reached over her arm to touch the kitten's head with gentle fingers. "Kind of makes me wish I were a cat," he teased.

She sent him a scathing stare then concentrated on the purring cat.

He chuckled at her response then his grin disappeared. "I'll try to start working on the yard week after next, if that's okay."

She knew firefighters were on-call 24/7, so a definite date and time would be impossible to lockdown. "Then I'll see you when I see you."

Despite her displeasure at their unexpected encounter, Francesca found herself admiring the way his suspenders stretched across his black t-shirt and broad shoulders as he walked away, his turnout coat draped over one arm. *We were good together once,* she thought and smiled as she remembered the major crush she had on him in high school when those shoulders wore football pads. Unbidden, memories of her first love came roaring back: the thrill of their first kiss at the Junior Prom, how proud she was to be the girlfriend of the captain of the football team, and how she loved it when he nicknamed her "Frankie," because he thought "Francesca" was too formal for "his tomboy girlfriend." Cody was still the only one who called her Frankie. In the heat of adolescent, puppy love, they'd sworn undying devotion to each other before they left Glen Eden heading in different directions to pursue college degrees. She'd gotten her Bachelor's degree in finance at Spring Hill University in Mobile, Alabama, and waited for him. He'd gotten a scholarship to play football at the University of Alabama, earned a Bachelor's degree in physical education, and married a college classmate.

"Yeah, that hurt," she murmured aloud, "but we were kids and that was a lifetime ago. When I think about it," she whispered into the kitten's ear then gave it a kiss, "I guess I kind of owe him for that. If we'd stayed together, I would never have gone on to law school."

On the way into the house with the purring kitten cradled in her arms, she realized where she could get the extra money to pay Cody. The judge she worked with was campaigning for re-election on next spring's primary ballot and had asked if she could take over some of his caseload. She decided she would dedicate that extra income to getting the yard cleaned up. And it would be a straightforward business deal. Money in one hand and out the other.

"Purr-fect," she trilled into the kitten's ear and planted another kiss on its head. "The Lord doth provide."

"DON'T START ON ME," Cody warned when he heard a chorus of "wooo-eee" as he walked into firehouse kitchen for a cup of coffee. He knew where the teasing was headed.

"What?" Joe Lyons said, with wide-eyed innocence. "Jonas told us the cat lady was an old flame of yours. We were thinking you must've handled that rescue all civil-like because there sure was a big grin on your face when you came back to the truck."

"No reason we can't be friendly. High school was a long time ago," Cody took a sip of the black brew before he poured it into the sink and followed that with the rest of the pot that tasted like it had been sitting on the burner all day. "Whoever left this on the burner needs to make the next pot."

"That would be the chief," Lyons said. "High school may have been a long time ago, but I've yet to meet a woman who wanted to still be friendly after being dumped."

Knowing it'd be wiser to make a fresh pot than to confront the chief about the burnt coffee, Cody got busy counting scoops of coffee grounds into a paper filter. "That's not what happened. We kind of grew apart is all." *There was no "we" involved*, he thought. *It was all me.*

"Betcha that's not what she thinks," Lyons said. "Did you really offer to work on her yard, and she agreed?"

"Like I said, no reason we can't be friendly."

"Is that what they're calling it nowadays?" Cal Jonas said. "Friendly? I saw how you looked at her."

"I admit I was thinking back on some good memories."

His heart ached when he realized how sweet those memories suddenly seemed. *I took a wrong turn in college*, he thought, *when I should've turned right . . . right back into Frankie's arms.*

"Doesn't hurt none that she's a squeezable, red-headed, five-foot-two cutie with green eyes either," Jonas teased.

"Cut it out, lech. Her hair is strawberry blond. Mostly she fosters cats, but right now she's also got a puppy that's had a hind leg amputated. Says it's going to get a prosthetic leg."

"I heard about them being able to do that," Lyons said around a mouthful of apple. "My wife is always on Facebook, and she was telling me something about it the other day."

"You thinking about trying to get back together with your cat lady?" Jonas said with a sly grin.

Cody sent him a head wobble and a one-shoulder shrug. "She's a good woman, and to paraphrase one of Flannery O'Connor's short stories, 'A good woman is hard to find.'"

Cody mentally chided himself for having to learn the hard way just how true that adage was. He examined the tiny, red scratch Muffin put on his arm and mused aloud, "I think I'd like a second chance."

THE BOLD HEADLINE OF the flyer read **Wanted: Fur-ever Home** over a picture of a black and white tuxedo kitten. Francesca picked the final sheet out of the printer tray and nodded in satisfaction. She'd used a computer program to modify the photo and now Tucker had a Santa hat on his head.

"The picture is adorable, even if I do say so myself." She stroked Tucker's silky coat. "You really do look like you're wearing your best bib and tucker. That's what my mom called a man's tuxedo, you know."

Francesca left the kitten snoozing on her desk, and with staple gun in hand, she tacked flyers on bulletin boards at Municipal Park, at the city's public pool, and at the sports complex fields. She wanted to attract the attention of the persons most responsible for the decision to adopt a pet—the kids in the family. Two hours later, she walked into the Pet Rescue Center and handed a flyer to the receptionist.

"Hi, Bobbie. Is it okay if I put one of my flyers on the board in your lobby?"

"A wanted poster," Bobbie said with a chuckle. "It's more than okay, Fran. It looks great. That red Santa hat makes his big, gold eyes stand out like neon lights."

"I'm hoping he'll be a precious, early Christmas gift for some lucky family."

"Did you post it on Facebook?"

"Nope. Too many strangers have access to Facebook. I want him to go to someone in town. Someone I can keep in contact with and know for sure they're treating him good."

"How are the fur babies doing?"

"They're great. Tucker's finally old enough to look for a forever home. Without any prompting, my neighbor claimed Niblet yesterday, and Muffin's a pistol. I had to call the fire department the other day to get her off the roof, and that caused me to run into Cody Phillips."

"How'd that go?"

"Is there some special meaning behind that question?"

"Sorry. I just wondered. He's been divorced for a while now, and I know you two used to be tight."

"That was high school. Let's leave it at that. It'll be couple of weeks before I can put Muffin up for adoption. That'll be tough, I'm about to get too attached to the little priss."

Bobbie chuckled. "Changing the subject are we? Okay, well, we have a solution for adoption anxiety. You need to take another foster."

"I keep telling you, I'm getting out of the fostering business. It's getting too hard to give them up, and yeah, I know. Fostering is all about doing what's best for the animal."

"Just thought I'd mention it."

"I wish you would stop baiting me. The last time you did that I wound up with a dog."

"How is Miss Molly?"

"Doing well with her physical therapy. She's been doing three sessions a week in the pool. The therapist said her muscle mass gets stronger with every visit, and her three legs are supporting her weight with no problem. She's a really sweet puppy, and believe it or not, the kittens have helped socialize her."

"I was worried about heartworm," Bobbie said, "because the mosquitos were thick this year, but good news. We got the results of the blood test yesterday, and she's heartworm negative."

"Prayers answered. And the prosthetic?"

"The manufacturer has the measurements, and it should be ready any day now. I'll send you an email when I've got it in the office, and we can set up an appointment with a technician to fit the device on the puppy."

AS SOON AS FRANCESCA walked into the house, an ecstatic Molly yipped and bounced and almost knocked her down. She captured the wriggling puppy in her arms and held her close while avoiding a barrage of wet puppy kisses. When the dog calmed down a bit, she let her go then dropped her purse, the few remaining flyers, and the day's mail on the kitchen counter. Her stomach sent out a hungry rumble as she freshened the food and water bowls—"for my critters" she said and nuzzled each one— then she made her own lunch. She used a fork to flake a can of albacore tuna into a dish, stirred in a dollop of light mayonnaise, a forkful of sweet pickle relish, and ate a bite before sitting down with a cup of black coffee. When her cell rang, she groped around in the bottom of her purse to find it before the call went to voice mail. Caller ID flashed a number she didn't recognize but thinking it might be a call about a forever home for Tucker, she answered with a hopeful "Hello?"

"Afternoon Frankie. It's me, Cody. Got a minute?"

"Hey, Cody. Are you already opting out of next weekend?"

"Nothing like that. I was thinking...wondering, if you're not seeing anyone special, would you like to join me for brunch at Brady's Buffet tomorrow after church?"

Is it the invitation, she wondered, or the sound of his voice? Whatever it was, it breathed life into a dark ember in the depths of her heart, and she tried, unsuccessfully, to stifle the heat it created.

"I didn't know you'd come back to church."

"Tomorrow is my first day back," he said. "It's time, don't you think?"

She bit back the snarky "yes" response that hovered on the tip of her tongue. "You've been missed," she said and was a bit surprised to find she meant it. "Everyone will be happy to see you again. Unfortunately, I have to decline your invitation for brunch." Her automatic refusal sent her mind racing for a good excuse, and she decided on: "There's no one special in my life right now, but one of the kittens is going to meet its forever family tomorrow."

"Next Sunday?"

When "Please don't ask me right now" leaped into her mind, she knew there might be a "yes" in the future, but she was nervous about going out with him again. Do I really want to try to reconnect and risk getting hurt again?

When she didn't answer for several seconds, he said. "That silence sounds like a 'no.'"

"It's just that Molly and the foster kitties don't leave me a lot of free time, Cody."

"Maybe next time," he said as if he'd read her mind. "See you at church then."

"Of course." When the call ended, she murmured, "Please forgive the lie about Tucker, Lord, but could you make it happen?"

The cellphone vibrated in her hand. She didn't recognize the ID name and number. "This better not be another robo call," she said before she answered.

Fifteen minutes later, she'd made an appointment to meet Tucker's potential forever family on Sunday afternoon. "Yessss," she hissed and pumped a fist. "Thank. You. Lord."

Without considering why it seemed important, she searched through the hangers in her closet to find something special to wear on Sunday. She sighed when she saw that everything there was from twenty-five pounds ago. Waiting to update her wardrobe until she reached her target of losing thirty pounds by New Year's Day no longer seemed like a good idea. She slid her hands down the front of an emerald-green, princess-style dress with no waist and decided it would be the easiest to alter to fit her new curves.

"Taking in a quick inch or two in the side seams is all it needs. Perfect," she said, then shook her head and added, "Why am I going to so much trouble? I'm only going to meet some cat people."

FRANCESCA WAS ONE OF the first to speak to Reverend Munson who waited in front of the sanctuary door to greet his congregation after the closing hymn ended. She was taking her first step off the small porch when Cody spoke softly into her ear: "That green dress looks great with your hair, makes you look all Christmas-y."

She unconsciously stood a bit straighter and her finger moved to the ruby crystal stud in her ear. "I think the Christmas season is way too short, so I exploit it as early as I can."

"Not as early as the stores do," he said and followed her down the steps. "It's not even Halloween, and I've already seen decorations for Thanksgiving and Christmas. New Year's Eve can't be far behind."

"I've done a few bankruptcies for small businesses," she said. "Stores have very narrow profit margins. A lot of them need good sales during those holidays to keep their bottom line in the black. Money truly is a demon taskmaster."

"It's always about the money," he said.

She understood from the sarcasm in his tone that her lame attempt at idle chatter had touched a nerve and decided it was time to leave.

"It's good to see you here this morning, Cody. Sorry I have to run, but I'm meeting a family about giving a kitten a second chance."

She spun away before the conversation could go any further.

Once home, her thoughts returned to her brusque reaction to Cody's overture. *I thought I'd forgiven him. I guess rejection is a lot harder to forget than I realized.* Away from the intensity of that moment, words from the minister's sermon chastised her: *Pray for a heart that forgives the worst, and a mind that forgets the bad.*

"Help me to move forward, Lord," she whispered.

FRANCESCA LEANED ON the open fridge door and studied the shelves for several minutes, trying to come up with something to cook for lunch that wouldn't leave a lingering smell throughout her house. Nothing inspired any ideas, so she opened a can of tomato soup and ate a small bowl of soup with a piece of warmed French bread with a smear of butter. When the doorbell rang two hours later, she got ready to meet the Hughes family. She put Muffin in her bedroom, Molly in the kennel, Tucker behind the bathroom door, and opened the door.

"Jacquie? My gosh," Francesca said and then wrapped her arms around her former high school classmate. "Why didn't you tell me it was you? I didn't know your married name."

"I wanted to surprise you."

"Well you certainly did that. Come on in. Now I know for sure Tucker will have a good home."

"This is my husband, Marlon, and my daughter, Jannis," Jacquie said and stroked her daughter's braids.

"I saw the wanted poster when I was leaving soccer practice at the park," ten-year-old Jannis said. "He's so cute. I just knew right away he was the kitty for me."

"We've been doing a tour of pet stores and breeders looking for a kitten to replace our fourteen-year-old yellow tabby," Marlon said.

"Marmalade died a month ago," Jacquie added, "and Jannis hasn't been able to shake her grief. Then she saw your kitten's picture, fell in love at first glance, and here we are,"

Francesca opened the door to the bathroom, and Tucker came prancing out, then crouched when he spotted strangers.

"Can I hold him?" Jannis said. "What kind of cat is he?"

"Let's wait to hold him until we see if he's okay with you. He's called a tuxedo because of his black and white markings."

Then Tucker seemed to decide the strangers posed no threat to him. He stretched out, laid one of his front paws on Jannis' sneaker as if bowing to her, then raised on his back legs and meowed.

"I think we have our answer," Francesca said. "He's begging you to pick him up." Jannis immediately swooped Tucker into her arms. While the little girl cuddled the kitten and cooed into his ear, Francesca sent her gaze toward the bemused mom and dad. "You're sure you want him?"

"There's no way we can say 'no' now that Jannis has him in her arms," Jacquie said with a laugh. "We want him," Jacquie and Ennis said, almost in unison, while Jannis' head bobbed up and down.

Francesca stroked Tucker's head. "Wonderful and exciting news, Sweetie. This marvelous family is going to give you a forever home. You be a good boy, okay?" Her throat began to ache and seemed to close as she planted a kiss between his ears. "I'll miss you," she said in a croaky voice.

She handed Jacquie a bag of kitten food, promised to call her for lunch, and gave Tucker's silky coat one last loving stroke before he left. When she shut the door behind them, she smiled in satisfaction, but the tears she'd been fighting back spilled over her lashes. Abruptly she swiped the wetness off her cheeks with her fingers.

"Enough. He's going to a good home. One down, two to go, and then no more." Even when she said it, she knew it was a lie. There'd always be one more sad and needy rescue she couldn't refuse.

She changed into jeans and a t-shirt and logged on to her email account.

The subject line on the first email read "Molly" and Francesca opened that one first.

"The prosthetic is ready," Bobbie's note read. "When can you bring Molly in for a fitting?"

"And so the adventure begins," she murmured with a smile.

"We'll be there tomorrow after work," she typed in the reply, hit send, and signed out.

FRANCESCA WATCHED ANXIOUSLY as Molly's prosthetic was fitted, removed, adjusted, and refitted again and
again until it was perfect in the technician's opinion. For her
part, the puppy calmly accepted all of the handling without a
yelp or a whimper. When the technician lifted her to a standing
position, Molly spent a brief time sniffing and examining the
strange attachment, before she tried a clumsy step. The prosthetic leg slid on the tile floor and threw Molly off balance.

"Oh, wow," Francesca cried. "Did we do the right thing?
That looks so painful."

The technician assured Francesca that Molly's first attempts at a stiff-legged walk were more painful for Francesca to
watch then it was for Molly.

"It'll take her a while to adapt. She'll do fine outside on the
grass and on carpeting," he said and moved Molly to a line of
carpet tiles where she took a few tentative but steadier steps.
"See? You'll need to lay down throw rugs on your tile or wood
floors."

The tech gave Francesca a list of do's and don'ts for Molly's
care, a warning about adverse symptoms and reactions, and
when to schedule a follow-up appointment to re-check the fitting.

"After that, there'll be several more sessions of physical
therapy," he said.

When Molly's initial confusion disappeared, she wriggled into and out of Francesca's arms and made an awkward move toward the door, ready to go home. Francesca crouched to pick her up, but the tech shook his head.

"Let her walk. After the newness wears off, she'll be fine. You'll be fine, too," he said with a reassuring smile.

"Maybe later, but not right now," she said and lifted the puppy into her arms.

BOBBIE AT THE PET RESCUE Center once again agreed to kennel Molly during the day and get her to the physical therapy sessions while Francesca was at work. Francesca was amazed at how quickly Molly became accustomed to the prosthetic leg. Two weeks after the fitting, Francesca and Molly were taking a morning walk when her cellphone vibrated, and she tapped into a phone message from Cody.

She combed the ruff of Molly's neck with her fingers. "Cody says he'll be here in about thirty minutes to finish the yard work," she said. "Today will be a twofer, sweetie. You get your walk, and I'll stop at the ATM to get some cash so we can pay him for his work. My Daddy—he would've loved you by the way—my Daddy always said one doesn't write an impersonal check when a friend does some work for you."

Forty minutes later Francesca was carrying the puppy home.

"It was a little too far, wasn't it, Sweetie."

She felt a little rush when she saw Cody's car parked in her driveway.

"Come on, Molly girl," Francesca said and set the puppy on the grass. "Let's go say 'hi' to Cody." The dog was already tugging on the leash.

"I was getting ready to break down the door," Cody said. "Your car is in the driveway, but you didn't answer when I knocked on the door several times."

"Sorry. I took Molly to the bank for her morning walk, and there was a man at the ATM who must've been doing a month's worth of transactions."

"It's Friday payday," he said. "I don't go near the bank or the grocery store on Friday or Saturday if I can help it."

Francesca rolled her eyes. "I do my banking electronically, so I forgot about it being exceptionally busy on payday."

"So this is Molly," he said and rubbed the puppy's ears.

"I forgot she was at the Rescue Center for her therapy session when you were here last week. You haven't met her yet. Well, here she is," Francesca said as she unclipped the leash from Molly who immediately took off after a bird. "And there she goes."

"Molly, the Wonder Dog. Look at her. She looks like she's grinning."

"Wonder Dog is a perfect description, and she grins all the time. Nothing seems to keep her down. Not even major surgery. When I took off her surgery cone, she looked around and seemed kind of surprised that her leg was missing, and that was that. "

"How old?" Cody said and chuckled as the wriggling puppy licked at his hand.

"About seven months near as we can tell."

"What kind of dog is she?"

"Vet said she's probably a beagle, and I can tell from the look on your face, you have no idea what I just said. It's a mix of beagle and golden retriever, She's got big paws though, so she won't be small like a beagle. Probably more of a medium-sized dog."

Molly walked back to Francesca and lay down next to her feet, her tongue flopped out of the side of her mouth, excited energy momentarily depleted.

Cody squatted to pet her then he ran his hand over the prosthetic. "This is amazing."

"They make them for all kinds of animals. I even saw a picture of an elephant fitted with a prosthetic leg. But the best one? The vet told me about a group of eighth graders who designed and 3D-printed a prosthetic foot for a disabled duck."

"You serious? Aren't eighth-graders about thirteen-years old? If those kids aren't walking on Mars in a few years, they'll be designing the equipment to get us there."

"And if I know you, you'll be first in line for a seat on the rocket." The banter sounded like old times, and she laughed.

"I've got some buddies who'd love to meet Molly," he said and ran his hand through the puppy's platinum-gold hair. "Can I take her with me sometime?"

"Sure. The more people she gets to meet, the better socialized she'll be. She's going up for adoption soon."

"Please don't let that happen before I call you. By the way, Glen Eden has a team competing in the county-wide Firefighter Challenge at Municipal Park next Saturday. Why don't you drop by? It wouldn't be like a date or anything. You'd be supporting all your local first responders."

"What's the challenge? A tug-of-war with fire hoses?"

"You're close. We'll be tugging against a ten-ton ladder truck—the chief got Montgomery to loan us one of theirs. Teams have to move the vehicle fifty feet using a hundred-foot rope. It's not just for firefighters, though. We challenged all comers, anyone who wants to participate—cops, gym junkies, whoever wants to put together a team. The rules restrict the teams to five people, and one of them has to be female. We even had a group of high school athletes register. Twenty teams have signed up so far, and the team with the fastest time wins."

He continued to pet Molly and when he looked up at Francesca, he reminded her of a kid petting his dog and excited about a game he was going to play, all bright-eyed and sweet and boyish and vulnerable. All the scars, foreign and domestic, kept hidden deep inside.

"That sounds like someone could get hurt."

"We'll have an ambulance standing by just in case, but mainly there'll just be a lot of sweating and grunting going on."

"And a lot of swearing, I bet."

"You'd lose that bet. It's a benefit event for the volunteer department in Deerfield Township. Plus, it's a way to do some public outreach. You know, introduce the community to who we are and what we do. Profanity doesn't play well at public relations events. By the way, I'm looking for pledges..." he said, his lifted voice leaving an opening in case she wanted to make one.

"Nice segue there," she said and laughed softly. "Sure, I'll pledge a dollar a foot and a fifty-dollar bonus if you win."

He gave Molly one last scratch beneath her chin and got to his feet.

"An even hundred. Very generous." Before she could dodge, he leaned close and brushed her cheek with a kiss. "Thank you."

Even after all those years, his touch was electric. "Now this one," she said and turned her other cheek. "In Europe, they kiss on both cheeks."

Cody took her by the shoulders and planted a wet kiss on both cheeks twice more. "In France, they say they know where you're from by counting the number of kisses," he said. "I think five is an appropriate number for Glen Eden, Alabama."

She wriggled out of his grasp and wiped the wetness off her cheeks.

"You nut," she said. "It's supposed to be an air kiss." Suddenly afraid she'd reawakened a long-buried emotion, she rushed to change the subject. "I always thought charity races, bike rides, chili cook-offs, and whatever happened in the spring."

"Think of this as a winter Olympics. The tires on Deerfield's pumper truck are pretty much bald, so they can't wait until spring. Me, three other regulars, and a volunteer firefighter have been weight training for weeks. Like I said, there has to be at least one female on the team, and our Julie is one tough firefighter."

Our Julie? The words chased away the warmth of his kiss. With a population of slightly more than fifty thousand taxpayers within the bedroom community's five square miles, Glen Eden's fire and rescue department had one fire station with two full-time crews and a dozen or so volunteers who rushed in when extra help was needed. Francesca thought she knew most of them, but "Julie" was a new name to her.

"I didn't know you had a woman firefighter at the station."

"We don't have one at the station. She's a volunteer."

The thought of another woman in a close relationship with Cody came with an unexpected jolt of jealousy. Francesca's mind whirled. *Is it more than professional? I didn't know he had a girlfriend. Why wouldn't he have a girlfriend? It's not like he's still married. I certainly don't have anything going with him.*

"I can get you a pass if you'd like to come," he said. "You'd have fun, and I could show off Molly to some of those friends I told you about. They'll be there, rooting me on."

You're more interested in Molly being there than me, she thought. *Of course you wouldn't want me there when you've got Julie.* She shook her head. "No free pass."

"You won't let me do anything for you."

The disappointment in his voice made her rethink her response. *Grow up, girl,* she thought. *You've no right to be jealous.*

"Don't get your knickers in a wad as Grandma used to say. The benefit can't make any money on free passes. I'll try to bring Molly by. That's all I can promise. I'll try."

IT WAS END OF SHIFT for Cody on the morning of the Firefighter Challenge, and he was awakened at the firehouse at five o'clock by the chiming of his cellphone alarm and the aroma of fresh coffee. He hit the showers and dressed in a hurry because the team planned to meet and prep for the Challenge at six a.m. at Municipal Park.

"Must be charity season," Lyons said while Cody filled his mouth with scrambled eggs and bites of whole wheat toast topped with a thick smear of grape jelly. "I read in the paper that there's going to be a 5K walk-and-run race benefiting the Pet Rescue Center in a couple of weeks. You gonna do that one?"

"Sure," Cody said and washed down his food with a gulp of strong coffee he had diluted and cooled down with a melting ice cube. "If you want to sponsor me with a twenty-five-buck pledge."

"You betcha, if you'll pledge fifty for me."

"In your dreams, Lyons."

"Why not? I have it on good authority that the Center provides Francesca DuBose with her rescues. Might improve your chances."

"Time to get our gear and go," Cody said and grabbed a bottle of orange juice out of his shift's fridge. "Don't want to be late for the TV cameras."

THE START OF THE FIRE truck towing event was still an hour away when Francesca dropped the ten-dollar fee into the shoebox at the entrance, and she and Molly walked into Municipal Park. The weather forecast said the day would be warm and humid with a possibility of rain so she'd dressed in chinos and a blue, Madras patchwork shirt with the sleeves rolled up. She carried her umbrella in a tote, together with a bottle of water to share with Molly. She began with a tour of the exhibits protected under tents. The aromas of hot dogs and funnel cakes lured her toward the food and beverage vendors that lined the perimeter of a grassy soccer field. A 100-foot long, red and white ladder truck with its ladder extended was parked near one of the goals. Kids and adults alike crawled in and out of ambulances and fire trucks of all sizes, parked with their doors open. EMTs and firefighters were in full public relations mode, explaining all the bells and whistles on the equipment and handing out red plastic helmets and badges to the kids. They also hawked chances to win a smoke alarm, fifty cents a ticket or three for a dollar.

"Hey look, Molly," Francesca said and petted the puppy's head. "It's one of the new smoke, fire, carbon monoxide combination alarms with ten-year batteries. We need one, don't we?"

She bought five dollars' worth of chances. "There's a prize winner in here someplace," she said to the firefighter selling the tickets then crouched, wrapped her arm around Molly's neck, and hugged her close.

"Molly girl, you're the best. It's downright peopley out here, and despite all the commotion, you're just as sweet and calm as a mama could hope for. I'll have a ton of adoption applications for you," she said.

She heard Cody call her name and turned to see him walking toward her wearing walnut brown hiking boots, black shorts, and a black t-shirt emblazoned with the fire department insignia and his name, "C. J. Phillips" on his chest. *I do love a man in uniform* she thought and got lost mapping the ripple of his sculpted chest muscles under the taut, knit t-shirt. She jumped like she'd gotten an electrical shock when he touched her.

"Glad you could make it," he said and took her hand. "Come on. I want to introduce you and show Molly off to my team." He slipped her hand over his arm and turned to the firefighter assisting with the ticket sales. "Everyone, this is Francesca DuBose and her wonder dog, Molly."

Molly, who had started to pant nervously, lay down next to Francesca's feet.

Cody put his hand on the shoulder of one of the firefighters who crouched next to Molly. "This is Sergeant Jerry Lyons."

"Nice to meet you," Lyons said and returned his attention to Molly's prosthetic leg.

Cody continued with the introductions of the rest of the firefighters gathered around Molly, and then pointed in the distance to a tall, brown woman with close-cropped, ebony curls.

"And over there, standing by our rig, is Julie Newman, our volunteer firefighter, and her husband Brad, who came along for moral support, I'm told."

"I thought . . ."

"Thought what?"

She felt her cheeks grow warm and wanted to melt into the dirt beneath her sneakers. "I mean ... I didn't think it would be so crowded. It's November and look how many people came out to support you. That ladder truck is huge. How much does that thing weigh?"

"Just shy of twenty-nine tons, but we're ready," Cody said with a grin and flexed a bicep.

The PA system blared, calling the teams to the starting area. Francesca was silently grateful it drowned out her lame backpedaling. She'd come close to publically embarrassing herself. She'd mistakenly presumed and prejudged Julie's relationship with Cody, the very things she fought against as an attorney.

"Good luck," she called as Cody and his team hurried away.

Francesca sat on the first tier of metal bleachers with Molly's head on her feet and watched each team make their two attempts and have their best time recorded in wide, blue letters on a huge, white board. Even though the best towing times were seconds long, the challenge took longer than she expected, and at a quarter after three, a misty rain started. When the teams took a break, waiting to see if the weather would clear, she decided to take Molly home to rest and to feed Muffin. She wanted to be back in time to watch Cody's team make their final pull, which could be the difference between a win and a loss for the squad from Glen Eden. They were in second place, but the course marshal had clocked them a three-second penalty for some kind infraction on their first pull. Worse, the penalty wouldn't be assessed until the competition was over. They'd have to win big in the final pull to overcome the penalty and have a chance at beating the first place team—Francesca didn't want to miss any of it.

WHEN FRANCESCA AND Molly stepped through the front door, Muffin scampered to greet them, all the while complaining about being left alone. While Francesca removed Molly's prosthetic so the puppy could lie down and rest comfortably, the kitten purred and groomed the dog's neck.

"That's sweet of you, Muffin. You missed your buddy, didn't you?"

Francesca refilled their water and food bowls, gave the foster babies a final hair mussing, and ran out of the house. The rain had stopped, and she'd be lucky to make it back to the park in time to see Cody's last truck pull.

She patted the steering column impatiently at the red light on the corner. When the light turned green, her foot hit the gas pedal faster than she intended, and the tires squealed into a jack rabbit start. Too late, she caught a glimpse of the car that ran a red light and hit her broadside.

"CODY, LET'S GO," LYONS yelled. "Rescue needs us on the truck for an extrication and wash-down. We got a two-car crash with the drivers trapped inside."

Adrenaline pushed his heart rate as Cody donned his turnout gear inside the cab while the driver headed toward the accident scene.

"This is one of the times I'm glad Glen Eden is so small," the driver said. "We'll be on-scene in just a couple of minutes."

When the driver braked to a stop, Cody and Lyons jogged towards the vehicles to assess what equipment they'd need to get the drivers to safety.

"This is no fender bender," Cody said when he saw the pickup with its nose buried in the passenger side of a minivan.

"Your basic T-bone accident," Lyons said. "Somebody ran a red light."

"If I didn't know she's at the truck tow right now, I'd say that's Frankie's minivan," Cody said and headed in that direction as Lyons turned toward the pickup.

Cody peered into the driver's window and his already racing heart skipped a beat. Francesca's face was buried in the air bag, her seat belt holding her limp body upright. Blood from a cut where her head had bounced off the side window trickled down her ashen cheek. He yanked savagely at her door handle, then the rear sliding door handle. Neither one budged. He broke the sliding door window and reached for the inside handle. The door still wouldn't open. He couldn't break her window without taking a chance on showering her with glass fragments. The engine compartment was throwing off steam, and he knew a gas spill from the carburetor onto the hot motor block could spark a fire. Francesca was trapped, and it would take the Jaws of Life to free her.

"Lyons! I need the Jaws. It's Frankie."

"Be there as soon as I can. We're using it on the pickup."

While the rest of the crew prepped to handle a fire if one broke out, Cody kept yanking on the door handles. "I'm here, Frankie. Hang on," Cody called repeatedly. "Only a few more minutes, and we'll have you free." Francesca didn't respond.

It was a long fifteen minutes until Lyons handed Cody the rescue tool. Cody wedged the tip of the jaws between the door and the van body and powered it up. He kept shoving and maneuvering the heavy tool, crunching and tearing at the screeching sheet metal until it gave way reluctantly. Lyons helped him peel back the door, then they stepped aside to let the EMTs take over. Francesca alternately moaned softly and answered the questions they asked as they wrapped a cervical collar around her neck and lifted her out of the crushed vehicle.

"This is the hardest part of this whole job," Cody said, his voice breaking.

Lyons nodded. "Not being able to do anything but watch is gut-wrenching."

"She's got a concussion, some bruising, and will be sore tomorrow, but otherwise, she's going to be fine," the ER doctor reported to Cody two hours later. "We're going to keep her overnight for observation of that head injury, though." Before Cody could ask, the doctor added, "You can see her as soon as they get her into her room. A-110, right down that hall."

Cody gently touched the big, white bandage on Francesca's forehead when the nurse left the room.

"You're going to have a black eye," he said and kissed her hand.

She grimaced. "It'll add to my character, don't you think?"

"I think you don't need any more character. What happened?"

"I was in a hurry, and no, I didn't run the red light. Hee did. But if I hadn't jumped the green without hesitating to look both ways, he probably would have missed me. They said the other driver is an old man. How is he?"

"Shaken up but going to be fine—probably because he's an old man. He wasn't driving very fast."

"I've got that to be thankful for. And you. I could hear you talking to me. Seemed like you were way off in the distance, but I heard you. Thanks for being there."

"Doing my job, rescuing cuties."

"I guess I needed a new van anyway. That one was ten years old."

"I've got a friend who can get you a deal on a car."

She shook her head in slow motion. "A van. I need a van for hauling the fosters and the kennels and stuff." She pushed the button on the remote to raise the head of the bed. "Can you put this bed rail down, so I can get up and get dressed? I don't care what the doctor said, I can't stay here overnight. Molly and Muffin—"

"You stay right where you are. I'll take care of Molly and Muffin. I still have the house key you gave me when I was working on the yard. And don't say no. Besides, you said your fur babies needed more socializing. I'll bring Molly to the cookout I'm having for some of my friends tonight," he said and grinned. "It'll be a perfect opportunity to see how she interacts with strangers when you're not around."

Her eyelids drooped. "I'm too tired to argue."

Her eyes were closed before she'd finished her sentence.

"I'll see you in the morning," Cody said and kissed her lightly on the cheek. "Love you," he whispered.

A tiny bit of a smile put a dimple in her cheek. "You, too."

"I DID NOT!"

"Did you change your mind overnight?"

"No. I mean...I couldn't have said that. I had a concussion."

The obvious confusion in his Cody's expression switched to an understanding smile. "You claiming mental incapacity?" he teased.

"Maybe I was talking in my sleep. That was it. I was probably dreaming about Molly, and I said 'I love you' to her. Not to you."

Cody's smile faded as he seemed to realize she wasn't teasing. "My bad. I guess I misunderstood," he said. "Okay, let's start this day over. You've been released from the hospital, and I, being a neighborly person with a fondness for cuties, am driving you home to your four-legged family. Would you like to stop for breakfast?"

"I'll pass, but thanks for asking. I'm ready to get into my own bed. Hospitals are no place to get any rest."

She was silent the rest of the way home. Despite her denials, she did remember hearing him say "Love you" and her "You, too" response. He'd stirred her emotions, and now, leery of being dumped again, she was afraid to admit how much she still cared for him.

For the first five minutes after Francesca walked in the front door, Molly was a wriggling and yipping ball of welcome-home energy, and Muffin wove figure eights around her ankles while she tried to walk toward her bedroom.

"C'mon, guys," she said with a giggle. "Let me go to bed."

Cody picked up the kitten and laid a calming hand on Molly's back.

"I'll take care of Molly and Muffin," he said. "You take as much time as you need."

Two days later, Francesca saw Cody's number flash on her cellphone while she was arranging for a loaner vehicle. After she'd talked the insurance adjuster into authorizing a minivan, she returned Cody's call.

He answered the call on the first ring with "Have you had lunch yet?"

"I had a late breakfast."

"Good, because I'm working on Doc Miller's yard right now, and I'm too dirty and sweaty to be seen in public. How about dinner? Give me a chance to go home and clean up. You still like Mario's spaghetti?"

"You're not going to give up are you?" she said, happy that he hadn't. She let out a melodramatic sigh and said, "Okay, yes. It's totally off my diet, but I still like Mario's spaghetti."

"Six-ish?" he said.

MARIO'S USED TO BE "the" place for high school teens to take their dates, but it faded out of favor as subsequent generations of students adopted new places to frequent. She hadn't been to Mario's since graduation, but the restaurant was as she remembered it: tables with shiny polyethylene finishes, empty Chianti wine bottles stoppered with candles dripping wax down the sides, deliciously mingled aromas of garlic and basil, and a low hum of conversations that bounced and echoed between the hard floors and high ceilings. A feeling of familiar comfort washed over her.

She stabbed her fork into the spaghetti, twirled the limber strands into her spoon, and slipped the lump into her mouth. She murmured a contented "yum" and continued to chew when Cody reached over and wiped a smear of tomato sauce off of her cheek. *Yes*, she thought as memories came flooding back. *This is exactly the way I remember it.*

"This used to be our go-to place," she said.

"This place and the frozen custard stand after football games. Those were the days."

"I think the operative word there is 'were.' You can't go back again."

"True, but you can start anew. Life is never really linear, except for the birth and death part. Things change. People change."

"I'm finding that out." She tore off a piece of bread and dipped it into a bowl of herbed olive oil. "A writer friend of mine says that when things don't go the way he planned or some disaster strikes, he yells, 'plot point' and changes direction. He says that way he never loses or fails, he simply sets a new goal and keeps moving forward."

"How about you, Frankie?"

Her pastor's words came back to her: *Pray for a heart that forgives the worst, and a mind that forgets the bad.* She examined the bread in her hand then dipped it deeper into the olive oil before answering.

"I'm good. I'm moving forward."

"You and I together were special. That once-in-a-lifetime kind of special that I . . . I didn't recognize until too late. A year into my marriage, I knew I'd made the biggest mistake of my life."

"Why didn't you divorce?"

"Using your friend's analogy, I guess Kathy was my plot point, but I didn't know how to change direction and not feel like a loser."

"You could never be a loser, Cody. You're too kind, thoughtful, and compassionate. You're all the things that make it easy for someone to take advantage and hurt you."

"Frankie, I ... Do you think you could ever forgive me...maybe be willing to give me a second chance? That's all I'm asking. A chance to make up for all the pain I caused you."

"I forgave you years ago, but that didn't mean I didn't hurt. I've avoided reconnecting with you out of pure self-defense. A second chance?"

She twirled spaghetti into a ball and stared at it for several seconds, then set down the fork and reached for his hand.

"I'd like that for us. A second chance for a happy ending."

He pressed her hand to his lips.

"Perfect timing," she said and laughed when the server took that moment to set their tiramisus and lattes in front of them.

"When are you planning to put Molly up for adoption?" Cody said when he was sipping the last of his latte.

"I printed off the flyers this morning."

"Are you sure you want to give her away? She's really sweet."

"I love it when a kitten I fostered is exactly what a family is looking for, that perfect piece that makes their family complete. Molly is my first foster puppy, and as much as I'd love to keep her, I have to do what's best for her."

Cody stared into his empty cup for a few minutes.

"I think I'm best." His voice picked up speed as if to stop her from protesting. "I checked with the VA. Because of her disability, she can't be a service dog for them. I can understand that. She might not be able to perform all the tasks her disabled owner requires. And she has extra needs herself. But I've seen how my friends light up when they see her. They love her, Frankie. She's one of them. She gives them hope, inspires them. With a little training, I think she'd make a wonderful therapy dog, and hospitals, even VA hospitals encourage therapy dog visits. Will you help me fill out the application?"

Francesca thought her heart would burst. Tears spilled down her cheeks, and she squealed with pleasure. "Oh my Lord, you're an answer to prayer," she said, ignoring the stares of the other customers. "Of course, I'll help you. I'll deliver it to Bobbie personally. You have no idea how much that means to me, Cody. With my other rescues, I didn't have the long getting-to-know-you period like I've had with Molly. I've come to love that puppy dearly and hated the thought that I'd have to give her up one day. Thank you, Cody. You've made me so very happy."

"While we're both on the happiness train, can I persuade you to adopt Muffin? If you're her forever hu-mom, she'll still be able to spend time with her favorite dog, 'cause I'll be asking you to dog-sit when I'm on duty at the station."

Francesca laughed. "You must've read my mind, because I had already decided I was the best family for her. I told the Rescue Center this morning I was going to adopt the little priss. Muffin and I will be very happy to have Molly with us while you're working."

Cody's eyes filled with tears, and he squeezed her hand.

"I want to spend the rest of my life making you happy, Frankie."

"I'd like to see you try," she said and with a feathery touch, brushed away the solitary tear that spilled over his long, black lashes onto his cheek. "You do know there'll always be more fosters, don't you?" When he laughed and nodded, she leaned close and whispered, "You're the final piece, Cody, the perfect piece to make my family complete."

About the Author

"Cj petterson" is the pen name of Marilyn A. Johnston who lives in historic Mobile, Alabama. She writes contemporary romantic suspense and mystery novels, and her non-fiction and fiction short stories have appeared in several anthologies.

A veteran of communication media in the corporate world, Marilyn began writing for pleasure as cj petterson after she retired from the auto industry and moved to the Gulf Coast. She is a member of Romance Writers of America, Sisters in Crime and their online Guppy group, Alabama Writers Conclave, Alabama Writers Forum, and a charter member of the Mobile Writers Guild.

Visit cj petterson on her blog at www.lyricalpens.com

And at cjpetterson/author on Facebook

Discover more of her work at

Simon&SchusterAuthor Page (http://bit.ly/2uo1M0Z[1])

AmazonCentral Author Page (http://amzn.to/1NID-KC0)

She invites you to sign up for her quarterly newsletter by writing to cjpetterson@gmail.com

---

1. http://bit.ly/2uo1M0Z%20

"Saving Grace"
By A.L. Vincent

A Bon Chance Boonie Short Story
For Furby

Grace hesitated a moment before sliding her key into the apartment door. She took a breath to calm herself before facing Gabe and his sweet but concerned eyes.

He always had that look when she came home from visiting with Dr. Melancon. As if he wanted to ask what they had talked about even though he already knew. These sessions had been his idea when her random outbursts of anger had almost caused them to break up at one point.

It was all Brent's fault, she thought. Although Dr. Mel had told her that it was reactive thinking and she needed to be proactive.

Grace rolled her eyes. Proactive would be driving to New Orleans, finding him and punching him in the throat.

She heard a bark from inside and knew she had been discovered. With a sigh, she opened the door and pasted a smile on her face.

Furby, the little white ball of fur she had rescued years ago came running up to her. His paws tip tapping on the hard wood floors of their small Austin apartment.

When he reached her, he jumped then did his welcome home dance on his back paws. She laughed then, as she always did, and picked him up. She buried her face in his soft fur and squeezed him tight. His presence a source of comfort at the end of a long and grueling day.

Gabe wandered in behind Furby, his lanky form filling the entry way. His green eyes were soft when he smiled at her. "He's been watching the door for you."

She held him out so she could look him in the eyes, "You did, Furb? You're such a good boy." With that, she placed him back down on the ground gently and he ran away. Back to the dog bed they'd placed between the sofa and the fireplace. He liked to turn it around so the high back faced the front. He looked like an overgrown rat defending the Queen's castle.

She hugged Gabe in greeting, then they kissed softly. As she stepped back, she saw his lips twist slightly with the effort of holding his questions back. Not wanting to start a conversation yet, she walked into the kitchen and fixed a drink.

She leaned back against the counter after she took a sip of the stiff vodka and Sprite, loving the burn that snaked down her throat. It felt better than the churning emotions her discussions with Dr. Mel always stirred up.

Gabe walked into the living room and turned on some music. She appreciated the soft sound of Marc Broussard as it floated through the apartment. His gravelly voice did as much to relax her as the alcohol did.

She exhaled then, feeling safe and comfortable at home. With Gabe.

She walked over to the stove where a big silver pot sat simmering. She lifted the lid, "Jambalaya. My favorite."

"Of course," he grinned, flashing devilish dimples. His look had softened a bit since they had stopped touring with the band. They were on a break now. Soon they would pack up and head back to their hometown of Bon Chance and then to New Orleans where they would attend a Christmas ball with Carly. How Grace had let Carly talk her into that nonsense, she'd never know.

Their good friend, Carly, was going with this new guy named Lucky. He was the cousin to Ryder, another one of their best friends. Knowing Ryder and his womanizing ways, Grace hoped that he wasn't cut from the same cloth. Carly had been through enough trauma in her life lately.

"What are you thinking about?" Gabe asked.

"Carly."

"Carly?"

"I was thinking about the ball next week."

"That's going to be fun, I think. Something different. And the Chateau Rouge is supposed to be haunted."

"That's the only reason I'm going," Grace said. "Dressing up is not my thing. But, some ghosts? Now I can get into that." She smiled then, her first real one of the night.

"I feel like I should get you a Ghostbuster outfit or something."

"Nah. I think I'll be good in my boots. They've served me well so far."

Gabe laughed, "Always the tough one."

"We'll see who's scared when push comes to shove and we're sleeping. Who's going to be sleeping with the lights on?"

"Is that a challenge?" he raised one dark eyebrow.

"It might be."

He started to move closer and involuntarily she stepped back. She cursed herself when she saw the hurt flare to life in his eyes. She hated herself for doing it. But more than that, she despised Brent for causing it all. One day, he was going to have to face the consequences for the damage he had done.

Gabe turned away and lifted the lid of the Magnalite pot on the stove, "I think the jambalaya is ready."

"I'm starving," she replied. And she was, it was amazing how fighting your inner demons worked up an appetite.

GRACE SHUDDERED AS Brent ran his cold fingers along her cheek.

"Remember me sweetheart?" he whispered in her ear. "I haven't forgotten you. And I'll be damned if I let you forget about me."

His fingers swept from her cheek to her collarbone, then traveled further down to the hemline of her top, his fingers like ice on her skin, "Or forget about this."

Grace sat up straight in bed, exhaling a silent scream. In response, Furby jumped up and barked furiously. Gabe slid out of bed and Grace could hear him in the kitchen, fixing her a glass of water. She was grateful that he gave her that moment to collect herself. The nightmares had abated over the past year, but when she dredged up some of those old memories at counseling they always came back.

He padded back into the bedroom, glass in hand. She took it with a smile. She sipped from the glass for a moment. She let the cold water wake her up and wash the memories away.

"Gabe?" she asked.

"Yes, babe?"

"Why don't we pack up today and head to Bon Chance?"

"I think that would be a great idea. I'll call Aunt Glinda."

"If we leave in the next hour, we can be there before sundown."

"Glinda will be excited to see us. I'll call Noah and Emily too. Maybe they can come have a drink with us."

"Sounds good."

She thought of their conversation the night before about Carly, "I know. Hey, why don't we make it a two-day trip and stop in Lafayette and see Carly? See how she's doing."

"We can do that. You start packing. I'll find us a room and make some reservations."

Grace climbed out of bed then and walked up to Gabe, wrapping her arms around him and placing a kiss on his lips.

"You're the best, you know that."

"You make it easy."

She laughed, "Liar. But you're sweet for saying so. I'm going to shower and pack."

"Do that. Let's go downtown again when we get to Lafayette. We had so much fun that night."

"Sounds perfect. A night of fun is exactly what I need right now."

"I think it will be great for us both. And Carly. And I need to check out this Lucky guy. See if he's anything like Ryder."

"Right?"

They both laughed before Grace gathered her things for her shower.

"Gabe?" she asked looking over her shoulder at him.

"Yeah, babe?"

"Have I ever told you how lucky I am to have you?"

"Grace?"

"Yes?"

He winked at her, "I am the lucky one."

She grinned, then closed the bathroom door.

"C'MON FURBY," GRACE said, attaching his leash. "We need to go for a walk before we get in the car. It's going to be a little trip. But you like that, don't ya buddy?"

He did a little turn after he was leashed and they walked out the door. The air was crisp, it was November, but it felt good on her face. Something about the chill made her feel more alive. After her counseling appointment and the reappearance of her nightmares, she needed to feel rejuvenated.

They were going back to New Orleans. The last time she was there, she had taken Brent's challenge and joined him on stage. She chose to sing about friendship, empowerment, and facing your fears. For a moment, she was in control. She was the one with the power.

How naive she was to think that it would be over that easily.

Lost in thought, she let Furby lead the way down the sidewalk. He pranced along, stopping here and there to sniff, or bark at another dog. It was a familiar route, so Grace wasn't too worried.

Suddenly, Furby jerked the leash, almost yanking it from her hand. Puzzled, Grace looked, but didn't see what had caught his attention.

Creeping closer, Grace's blood ran cold. A rattlesnake lay curled in the bushes by the sidewalk.

"No, Furby, get back," she said, pulling his leash. She resisted the urge to rush to pick him up for fear she would startle the snake and make him strike.

Slowly she pulled him back, while reaching for the knife she kept at her ankle.

The snake slowly rose its head. Furby lunged one more time. She curled the knife in her hand, ready to strike. She threw the weapon at the snake, aiming for its head.

Furby's howl of pain pierced the quiet morning. She ran to the dog who laid crumpled on the cold concrete.

The snake, impaled on her knife, still twisted.

In a blind rage, she pulled the knife out of the snake, and cut its head off. The movement stopped and the immediate danger was eliminated.

Furby whimpered and she gently curled him against her chest. He panted softly, and fear ran through her veins like ice.

He couldn't die. Not Furby.

She took off at a dead run, her only thought getting Furby to the vet. He had to be okay. He just had to.

"GABE!" SHE SHOUTED as she burst into the door, "It's Furby!" Her voice broke as she said, "He's hurt!"

Gabe rushed out of the bedroom. "What is it? Did he get hit by a car?"

"No, a rattlesnake bite! Hurry, Gabe! We have to get him to the vet!"

Furby whimpered, and a tear fell down Grace's cheek. Gabe reached out for her and hugged her, careful not to squeeze the little dog.

"Let me get my keys. Call the vet on the way."

Grace continued to hold Furby, whispering words of comfort. As much for her benefit as his.

Gabe returned with his keys and a small towel. Grace carefully wrapped him in the soft fabric and they hurried out the door. The wind blew cold across her tear dampened cheeks.

The town of Austin sped by in a watery blur. Grace saw nothing of the town's unique personality or the recent addition of bright Christmas decorations.

Grace's door was open and she was sliding out before the truck rolled to a complete stop. She sprinted into the vet's office where Liz, one of the technicians was already waiting. They took the shivering dog and rushed him into an exam room.

"Poor baby," she said stroking his back, being careful not to touch his face that was swelling.

Furby's body went stiff on the table and Gabe had to reach out to keep Grace from falling as her knees buckled. Liz left the room, returning quickly with Dr. David.

He quickly assessed the dog, patting him tenderly as the dog continued to seize. As Furby came to, the doctor began to gently look over the dog.

"Yeah, that's some snakebite. Did you see the snake?"

"Yes, it was a rattlesnake. A smallish one."

"Since I know what we're working with I know what anti-venom we need. We're going to keep him overnight. He'll need an IV. And we want to keep him as still as possible and watch him for any complications."

"Will he be okay?"

"You got him here pretty quick. That's always good. Dogs have a good chance of surviving a snakebite when they receive prompt medical attention."

Liz picked Furby up and held him against her chest, "Do you want to give him a little goodbye before I take him back?"

"Yes,"

Grace fought tears as she patted his little head, "You're going to be okay, all right? You just hang in there."

His little brown eyes blinked and he licked her hand. Grace sniffed and smiled, "Good boy. We'll see you tomorrow, okay?"

She watched as they left through the door. She clutched Gabe's hand.

"You heard him, he has a good chance. He's in good hands now. Let's go home. I already sent Carly and Aunt Glinda texts to let them know that we wouldn't be leaving today, so don't worry about that."

Gabe wrapped his arm around her as they walked outside. She took comfort in his warm and steady presence. "I'm going to take care of you today. Whatever you want, it's yours."

"I just want Furby to be okay."

"I know."

The ride home was relatively quiet, the only sound was the music playing quietly on the radio.

GRACE CHANGED INTO leggings and one of Gabe's tour t-shirts and curled up on the sofa. She avoided looking at the empty dog bed that lay by the fireplace.

Gabe came in with two drinks. He handed her one, then sat down at the end of the sofa. Grace stretched out and rested her socked feet on his legs. He placed one hand on her ankle, and grabbed the remote with the other, "Any requests?"

"I don't care. Anything." They had similar tastes in television shows so she could trust him to pick something they would both enjoy. He settled on a crime drama. As the familiar storyline played on the screen, Grace thought about how she had found Furby all those years ago after a gig in New Orleans.

Hot and sweaty from the night's performance, Grace welcomed the fresh air as she stepped out of the night club's back entrance and into the back alley of Bourbon Street. The area was lit by only a flickering streetlight, but Grace was not scared. She had a knife tucked into the side of her black leather boot, and she was not afraid to use it. With the hours she kept, walking the Quar-

ter wasn't the safest of places, the weapon made her feel safer when out all alone.

A low growl made her stop and look around. A huge black dog had found a possible meal in a trash bag that had fallen and ripped open.

Standing between the food and the bag was a small white scrap of fur. He bared his teeth in response, willing to take on the bigger dog in a show that Grace found impressive. Stupid. But, impressive.

She whistled, gaining the attention of both dogs. When they paused, she went over and scooped up the trembling smaller mutt. The dog stunk to high heaven, and she held him out by the scruff of his neck before unzipping her backpack and stuffing him inside, leaving his little matted head poking out. He growled again at the other dog, but the other animal was occupied by the garbage and paid him no mind.

"Hush, you," she said. What was she going to do now? She didn't need a dog. She worked too much for that responsibility. He would need to be walked and fed. Maybe she should take him to animal control when they opened. Surely, he would be happier there than on the streets. He would have a roof over his head and meals. They could find him a home.

Tonight though, he would need food and the various accessories that came along with a dog. And shampoo. The dog smelled like the dumpster he was just rummaging in.

There was a CVS on the way home, she would stop in there and pick a few things up. Just enough to last until she could take him to the shelter.

She sang softly to herself while she walked through the bustling streets of the French Quarter to her apartment. She could feel the dog relax against her back. She smiled to herself when he poked his head out and sniffed as they walked by a Lucky Dog stand.

"You're the Lucky Dog tonight, cher. *I saved you from almost certain death."*

She reached behind and patted his head. She wondered if he would let her try to brush him or cut some of the tangles out to make him more comfortable.

"Shh," she told him as they walked into the CVS. With any luck no one would notice him. No one took much notice of a woman with a backpack in New Orleans. There were so many other things that would catch your attention. She walked quickly through the aisles, grabbing a small bag of food, a leash, collar, some shampoo, and a small fuzzy toy.

After that, her last stop of the night was part of her normal routine, a small place open 24 hours. She stopped in for a cup of coffee and an order of beignets. She ordered a side of bacon for the dog.

When she got to the apartment she shared with a college student, she took the dog out of her backpack and put the new leash and collar on him so she could walk him around for a bit before taking him in.

"First, food." She grabbed an old bowl and filled it with the dog food. The dog ran to it, eating as if his life depended on it. Maybe it had.

Grace sipped her coffee and munched on the sugary beignet while the dog ate. He had pretty white fur with a few brown spots, and hazel eyes that took in everything around him. He would probably be a cute little thing when he was cleaned up.

While she waited for him to finish eating, she scrolled through her phone, killing time. She looked down when she realized he was quiet and smiled when she saw him sleeping in his food dish. She didn't have the heart to wake him, so let him lay there. His belly full, finally able to rest.

GRACE AWOKE TO THE sound of her phone ringing. Her heart raced when she saw the caller, it was the vet. Breathlessly, she answered the phone, "Hello."

"Ms. Delchamp? This is Liz from Dr. David's office. Furby is ready for you to pick him up."

Grace sagged against the sofa she had fallen asleep on, "Thank God," she said. Her voice still raspy with sleep. Gabe roused from his spot on the couch too, he smiled and rubbed her leg. They had stayed up late, staring at the TV while a favorite show played on Netflix. Exhausted, Grace had finally drifted off around dawn.

She reached out for him, "He's okay. We can go get him."

Gabe hugged her close and kissed the top of her head, "Let's go then."

Moments later, they were in the car, heading to the vet. The attendant smiled as they came in, "Can I help you?"

"I'm here to pick up Furby."

"We'll have him out in a moment."

Grace, unable to sit still, paced the small lobby, six steps forward, six steps back. She counted as she waited for them to bring her baby to the front.

She detected movement, and the tech was there with Furby. She reached out for Gabriel's hand, and he took it and squeezed. When Liz handed Furby over, Grace cuddled him to her chest.

He was going to be okay.

"He's going to be a little out of it for the next 24-48 hours," the tech said. "He's still in some pain, but he's made it through the worst of it."

"Thank you," Grace said, fighting off tears. She reached for her wallet.

Gabe reached out and touched her hand, "I've got this."

Grace took a deep breath and smiled at him, while hugging her dog close. Furby snuggled into her arms and closed his eyes. He wasn't his normal feisty self. But, he was going to be okay.

GABE OPENED THE FRONT door for them. Realizing he was home, Furby responded with a weak wag of his tail. Grace squeezed him lightly, then set him down on the floor when they entered the living room. He slowly made his way to his bed by the fireplace and curled up in a ball.

"He's home," Grace said with a sigh. Gabe reached out and pulled her into a tight hug.

"Yes, he is. How about I warm up some jambalaya. We can watch some TV and you can keep watch on the Furbster."

"That sounds incredible. Thank you."

Grace took the seat closest to the dog bed and grabbed the remote. She clicked through channels until she found a ghost hunter show. Since they were staying in a "haunted" hotel in a few days...*Might as well*, she thought.

Furby let out a small groan and she looked down at him. Then she looked at the time. It was still a couple of hours before she would need to give him another dose of pain meds. She leaned down and stroked his fur, and he relaxed and fell back asleep.

Grace remembered when she had stirred in her sleep after Brent. When her dreams haunted her, and she tossed and turned. It was Furby who curled up by her head, laying his little head next to hers.

Wounded. They were both wounded. Only Grace's scars could not be seen. She exhaled a breath.

Recovery was a bitch.

GRACE ROLLED THE WINDOW down as they began crossing the long bridge into Bon Chance. It would be a bit of a drive over marshland, but for miles and miles it was nothing but blue water, sea gulls, and the salty welcoming scent of home.

Furby tapped his tail against the floorboard as he sniffed in the air. He'd have room to run along the beach, and lots of treats from Aunt Glinda.

Gabe looked over at her and placed his hand over hers. She took comfort in the warmth. The wind rushing into the cab of the truck had the slight bite of winter.

"I wonder if Glinda has the tree decorated yet?" Gabe asked.

"I hope not. We didn't put a tree up this year. It would be nice to do. We could drink some eggnog, listen to some Christmas tunes."

Stuff that normal couples did. Stuff that Grace wished they could get back to. She drew the line though at hot chocolate and Hallmark movies.

That should be a song title, she thought. Her lips curling slightly in a smile.

"Christmas Eve is coming soon. Have you thought of what you want Santa to bring you for Christmas?"

Grace rolled her eyes, "We are not starting this."

"Ah now. I know you've already got a few things in that bag for the Furbster."

She did, a couple of new chew toys and treats. She hadn't bought Gabe anything yet. She felt guilty, but nothing just seemed quite *right* yet. Maybe she and Carly would find something in New Orleans. There seemed to be something for everyone there.

The highway turned and the town came into view. Grace sat back and enjoyed the familiar sights of the fishing camps and businesses.

They stopped in front of the empty lot that used to be Snapper's. It was only a blank slab of concrete now. Grace's heart constricted, thinking of the memories there, both good and bad.

She reached out for Gabriel, thinking of Carly. This place had been such a big part of her life for so long. It must have hit her harder than she expected.

"Do you think she's seen this?" Grace asked.

"I don't know."

"Noah would know. I'm sure him and Emily will come for dinner tonight."

"I hope so. I've been missing some of Emily's cooking."

"It will be good to see them again. It's been a while."

After Grace had left her teaching job and went to Austin with Gabe, it had been nonstop touring. They had opened for some great bands and had three hits of their own.

Her eyes clouded over for a moment.

"What is it?" Gabe said.

"Just thinking."

He nudged her a bit, "About what?"

"About the time I sang. When I threw up after."

He hugged her close but didn't say anything. She loved that about him. He didn't pressure her. Or worse, tell her that things would get better. Or that was in the past. Or any other trite comment.

He kissed the top of her head, "Let's go. Glinda's probably waiting for us on the porch by now."

She looked around once more at the empty space. "Alright, but you get to make the first drink."

"But, of course my *cher*. Whatever you want."

SURE ENOUGH, GLINDA and Daniel were sitting on the large front porch of the Redbird Inn. Glinda stood as they drove up, placing a hand-made blanket in the chair as she stood up.

She waved, and the two hounds raised their heads in greeting. One barked, but that would be the most energy they would expend until it was time to go in.

"Hi Aunt Glinda!" Gabe said, raising his hand too.

She walked down the steps to greet them both with hugs. "Oh, it's so good to see you two! Noah and Emily are coming later. So is Joey. Oh, that boy has just been beside himself since Carly left. I don't know why he just doesn't load himself up and go to Lafayette."

Gabe grinned, "Oh, I don't know, Aunt Glinda. I'm sure he has his reasons."

"Well, not any that make any sense. Y'all come on in. Fix yourselves a drink. I have some gumbo simmering on the stove. Emily is bringing the potato salad and the rest in about an hour. If you're hungry now, there's a cheese board on the bar." She ushered them into the house.

Gabe and Grace hugged and greeted Daniel.

"Oh I can't wait to see the pictures of you all, dressed up and all at that ball. You are going to be just gorgeous. Daniel and I are coming up too. We're not doing the ball, of course, but we've made it a tradition to go up there and take in all the lights. It's so pretty this time of year."

"Yes, it is," Grace agreed. It was her favorite time in New Orleans. It was the opposite of Mardi Gras. The crowds, the mess, the smell. She did not miss that about her old home. Christmas was cold and crisp. They sang carols in the Quarter near the Cathedral and the hotels decked themselves out. She was actually looking forward to strolling down the streets and popping in to the different businesses and seeing the lavish decorations.

As they walked into the large main area of the bed and breakfast, Grace was glad to see that the tree was up, but not yet decorated. It was fresh and the scent of pine permeated the room.

"I figured you guys could help me out with the tree this year. Carly usually does, but..." Glinda trailed off. It seemed Joey wasn't the only one who missed Carly.

"We'll be happy to," Grace said. "In fact, I was hoping that you hadn't. We didn't put up a tree this year, and now I kind of regret it."

"Well, girl, you get yourselves a drink and see what I have. The storage containers are there. I'm going to finish up in the kitchen.

"I'll help," Daniel said as he followed her into the other room.

While Gabriel fixed them a drink, Grace started perusing the containers. Furby watched from his spot on a throw blanket on the sofa. She was pulling out the strands of white lights when Gabe brought her a drink.

"Thank you."

"My pleasure. So, what all do we have here?"

"We have it all, lights, ornaments, some tinsel."

"Don't get your tinsel in a tangle," he said smiling and kissing her softly.

She laughed, "You're so corny."

"But it made you smile."

"That it did."

"Let me go put on some music, and then I'll be back to help."

"Awesome." Grace started stringing the lights through the tree. She smiled when Christmas carols began drifting through the room. "Doing this right, I see."

"Of course." He reached out for the strands of lights, "Let me help."

Together they wrapped the lights around the tree, when they finished they plugged them in and admired their handiwork.

"Clear lights are my favorite," Grace said. "So simple."

Gabe walked up behind her and wrapped his arms around her waist. He placed his chin on top of her head. She leaned into him, "This is perfect. Exactly what I needed."

She looked around at the familiar Redbird Inn, where she had eaten countless meals. She thought about the beach just across the road where she had started to heal. It was this place that centered her. That gave her strength.

She turned in Gabe's arms, looking him in the eye, "I love you, you know that?"

He kissed her on the forehead before responding, "I know. And I love you too. Always have. Always will."

Grace rested her head on his shoulders. As she did, "Have Yourself a Merry Little Christmas" began to play.

He reached out for her hand, "Come on. Dance with me."

He led her to the spot in front of the fireplace, and together they swayed to the music. She wasn't one to be overly sentimental, but if there was anyone who deserved a merry little Christmas, it was her.

"HOW DID YOU DO IT, Emily?" Grace asked. After dinner the group had returned to the family room. Gabriel and Emily's boyfriend, Noah, were enjoying a drink and a friendly game of pool. The two women had taken spots in the two big chairs by the fire.

"What do you mean?" Emily's brown eyes were questioning.

"Your husband was an asshole. How did you let that go?"

"When he tried to ruin the spaghetti cook-off for me, I was so mad. But, I realized that he wasn't worth it. I had so many good things going on, like Noah, coming back here, and new projects coming up." Emily took a sip of her drink before continuing. "I remember one day I was seasoning Ruby's old cast iron pot. Carly ended up coming over and somehow it just turned into a party. It made me think of how the people made my life so much better. It focused me on the good things."

Grace nodded, "That's a good way to look at it."

"Eddie was nowhere near what happened to you. An asshole, yes, but he wasn't always that way, and he really didn't do anything outright malicious. It was the alcohol. Not that that excuses him in any way. But, if you don't let that anger go, it will continue to flicker and eventually it may even burn the good stuff away."

"I know. It's just hard to leave it behind me. Grace stopped and stared at the fireplace for a moment before continuing, "You know, Noah once said to me that there are some things you can't outrun. Maybe it's time I stopped running."

Emily nodded, "You are going back to New Orleans tomorrow. That's where it all started. Maybe," she grinned and nodded at Gabe. "Maybe you can figure out new beginning."

Grace raised her glass toward Emily, "You may be right, my friend. You may be right."

THE BRUNCH PLACE CARLY had suggested was already bustling with people. Always a good sign. A waitress greeted them quickly and soon they were seated. Their orders for mimosas were taken and they perused the menu. They had left the guys back at the hotel to spend the morning doing some Christmas shopping in the French Quarter.

"So tell me about everything that's going on! I still can't believe you got to meet Aaron Lewis! I was so jealous!"

"He was a cool guy. Very nice. Down to earth. I have to say it was a highlight of our tour."

"And next year? What do you guys have planned?"

"I don't know yet. We don't have another tour scheduled yet. It looks like some down time to write is on the agenda."

The waitress returned with their drinks and took their orders.

Grace resisted the urge to ask Carly how she was really feeling about Joey, about the move to Lafayette, about the loss of Snapper's. Grace knew enough of what those questions felt like. Carly would share when she was ready.

"Tell me about this new book project," Grace said instead.

Carly's face lit up like the proverbial Christmas tree. "Ohmygod Grace! It's been so cool! It started with meeting Dawn. She's a best-selling author! Well, she read my stuff. Told me it was crap."

Grace raised an eyebrow.

"No, no." Carly continued, "She was right. It was crap. So I scrapped it all. Get it? Scrapped the crap?"

Grace gazed at her over the rim of the glass she'd just raised to her lips to keep from groaning.

"I get it. I hope that's not the title of your next book. However, as I look back on your love life..."

"Ha ha." Carly said, rolling her eyes.

"Anyway. I went with Lucky to Biloxi. Speaking of my love life.

"Please tell me you didn't take a man named Lucky to a casino."

"I did! And I ran into A.J."

"The ex-fiancé?" Now, Carly was spilling the good stuff.

"Yes! And it was awesome! I was looking good. Lucky was looking good. I was happy. It was like the last few years disappeared. I looked him in the eye. And I asked myself, what was it that had kept me angry for so long? And I let it go."

Grace, who had been about to take another sip of her drink, nearly spit it out all over the table.

What would it be like to face off with Brent? She had had a moment in New Orleans where she had shared a stage with him again, but it had only fueled her fire. It hadn't calmed her rage. That anger that still bubbled just underneath the surface.

Would that be what it took to finally let it go herself? And what would she even say? There weren't enough words she could say to erase the pain she felt.

"Grace? You okay?" Carly asked.

Grace brushed aside her thoughts for now and concentrated on her friend. Emily was right about one thing. It was friends that were important.

"I CAN'T BELIEVE YOU bought Furby gifts, but you haven't bought anything yet for Gabe." Carly chided as they walked down the busy bricked sidewalks of the French Quarter.

"Furby's easy. You buy him some chew toys and he's good. I highly doubt Gabe would be happy with a squeaky toy and a pat on the head. It's hard to buy for him."

"Well, the bartender said this place should have the perfect gift. *Enchantee*. Sounds expensive." Carly said. She eyed the name on the door, and it's scrolling gold lettering. "Looks expensive too. Hope you brought your credit card."

The door chimed as they walked in. A woman stepped out from behind a beaded curtain.

"Good afternoon," she said in an old-world accent that mirrored the bartender's.

"Hi!" Carly said, "We're doing some Christmas shopping. Ivy at the Chateau Rouge said we should be able to find the perfect gift. And she said you were the person to go to for a card reading."

The woman smiled, "Ah yes, Ivy sent you. Come on in. Will you both be getting a reading?"

Carly looked over at Grace, "Oh come on. It will be fun."

Grace wasn't sure she wanted someone poking around in her brain. She had already experienced about enough of that. But what was it Carly said, "Let it go?" Damn, she was starting to sound like an overplayed Disney song.

"Why not?" This whole weekend was to get her out of her comfort zone and try new things. "But, you go first."

Carly beamed, "We'll be getting two readings today."

"Call me Madam Vivian."

Grace resisted the urge to roll her eyes. Madam Vivian. Must everyone in New Orleans play some kind of role? This was why Grace had avoided most touristy spots when she lived here.

"Come ladies," Vivian gestured to a small table in the corner of the room. A stack of black tarot cards rested beside a burning candle.

"Please have a seat."

Carly took a seat. Grace, feeling restless said, "I'm going to look around. I still need to get that gift for Gabe."

Vivian began giving Carly directions as Grace wandered away. The bartender at the Chateau Rouge had been right, the store was a treasure trove of unique items. A collection of ornate skeleton keys caught her eye. Keys opened doors. Doors represented new possibilities. What was it that old adage said, "When one door closes, another one opens?" It was kind of a feminine gift, but she picked one up with red jewel inside its heart shaped end.

"Your turn!" Carly said, returning. "Oh my God, she's good. I can't wait to tell you what she read for me."

"Sounds like a good lunch conversation."

"Definitely, now go get yours read."

Grace was relieved when Carly seemed to be content to give her some space and privacy as she sat to get her own reading done.

The woman pushed the cards toward her, "Shuffle the cards until you feel like stopping."

Grace took the worn cards in her hands and did as directed. When she felt like they had been mixed up enough, she slid the cards back to Vivian, who laid them out in a spread.

"The first card is the hermit. You have a lot on your mind right now. You are looking for answers to questions and you have no idea where to turn. But, what you want is a new beginning. A fresh start. You crave a new path. But you don't know where to go or how to get here."

Grace was surprised this woman was so accurate so far, but she kept her expression blank.

Vivian continued, motioning to a picture of a bright yellow sun, "The sun heralds a new day, a new happiness. It's a time to start a new venture."

If only I knew what that was, Grace thought.

"The Wheel of Fortune means 'what comes around, goes around,'" and is a time of karma. You get what you give."

I'd like to see karma bite Brent in the behind. Grace resisted the urge to smile.

"The last two cards are the moon and the high priestess. Stop living in fear and insecurity. Trust that all will turn out well in the end. Look for the moon to bring new and promising opportunities."

Vivian gestured to all the cards, "Whatever darkness you've experienced is behind you. You are the person holding yourself back. You have the sun on your side. It's up to you to take that next step. But, you don't strike me as a person to listen to what some cards say. You know what you need to do. Now, do it."

Grace liked the woman's frank nature. Next time she was in town, she'd definitely have to pay *Enchantee* another visit. "Thank you for the reading."

"You're welcome, *cher*."

The two women paid for their readings and purchases, "I don't know about you, Carly," Grace said. "But, I need a drink after that."

"Lead on. I'm sure we can find someplace around here." Carly laughed as she pushed the door open and they stepped back on the busy streets of the French Quarter.

AFTER THE CHRISTMAS Ball, Grace flipped through the channels of the TV. Gabe lay beside her, snoring softly. Furby lay on his back in between them, not a care in the world. Grace had originally planned to leave the dog in Bon Chance with Glinda, but had changed her mind at the last minute, unwilling to let him out of her sight for too long. Going to the ball for those few hours had been long enough. In the light of the TV, she could see the wound that was still healing on his face.

She blew out a breath and sat up in bed. Quietly, she grabbed her jeans and shoes.

I hope the bar is still open, she thought as she hit the button on the elevator.

A few moments later, she was in the lobby of the hotel, soft piano music played softly from the bar. The dim lights signaling it was still open. Grace walked in and grabbed a seat. She nodded to the red headed bartender, Ivy, who was drinking a glass of wine at the end of the bar. The bartender took her order for a vodka tonic and left Grace alone with her thoughts.

"Uh oh, that look has 'man' written all over it," Ivy said as she slid onto a seat beside Grace.

Grace rose an eyebrow but didn't respond.

"Want to talk about it? People love telling bartenders their stories." She lit a clove cigarette, the spicy scent permeating the room, "Want one?" She held out a silver cigarette holder.

"Why not?" She lit the cigarette, "I thought New Orleans was a no-smoking town."

Ivy laughed, "I hardly think anyone will tell me anything in this bar."

"All right then. "But, you're no bartender, tonight anyway."

"True," she paused and took a sip from her glass. "It's not that hunky man you were at the ball with earlier is it?"

Grace smiled, "No, not Gabe. Just some nightmares of the past."

"Then boo, I wouldn't let the past keep me out of that bed," Ivy grinned. "Seems like a wasted opportunity. You down here. Him up in bed. He's almost too tasty resist."

There was a distance between her and Gabriel that hadn't been there since she'd returned to Bon Chance the morning after she'd woken up with Brent with no memory of what happened.

Grace resisted the urge to sigh. That train of thought would lead her nowhere. She had hoped this getaway would heal that divide between them. Instead, she felt farther away from him than ever.

Here she was again, stuck in the past, unable to move forward. Seems life had a way of repeating itself. She was here once again to escape the ghost of Brent.

"It's just some old ghosts," she said to Ivy.

Ivy laughed then, "Girl, this hotel, this town is full of ghosts. You know what? They're dead. There's nothing they can do to you."

"You know, you're right about that," Grace took a last sip of her drink and stubbed out the cigarette. Thanks, Ivy. I think I'm going to take a little walk now. I think that should clear out any 'ghosts.'"

Ivy nodded, "Here, take a cig for the road. I've always found a good smoke after chasing off ghosts to be quite satisfying."

Grace nodded and tucked the cigarette safely in her wallet.

"Have a good rest of your evening," Grace said. Ivy nodded and Grace walked out of the bar and into the night.

She wandered through the French Quarter aimlessly. Memories flashed through her mind like a montage in a movie. The upbeat jazz music coming from the clubs was a contrast to what was going on her head.

Her first stop was her old apartment. She stood outside on the sidewalk, looking up to what used to be her window. Her roommate had graduated and moved out, and new people resided there. More new beginnings.

"I let it go..." Carly's voice sounded in her head again. Grace stood there silently for a moment. Reminding herself of the good that had happened in that apartment. The laughter with her roommate. The late nights and early mornings of music, cooking, and binge watching *The Originals*. The good times.

Grace smiled, feeling some of the old anger that had been her constant companion for too long slowly fade away. She nodded her head. She had one more stop to make.

She heard his voice as she got closer to the club where she knew they would be playing. She waited for the old anxiety to kick in, and was relieved when it didn't. She stepped in, stopping in the doorway for a moment. The band was halfway through a rendition of "Pour Some Sugar on Me."

It was a fan favorite and many patrons were singing along. Grace remembered when she had been up there with him, playing to the crowd, getting them to participate.

It was also the last song in their set. Soon, they would wrap up, pack up, and be on their way. What would she say if she waited for him out in that dark alley? Would she yell at him?

Scream what he did to her at the top of her lungs for anyone to hear? Call him every foul name she had ever thought of him?

She turned from the doorway, walking around the corner to the entrance of the alley. It was time to find out.

GRACE LEANED AGAINST the back wall, one leg up. She watched the door. She thought of the snake that had bitten Furby only a few days before. It had curled up and laid in wait for prey to walk by. Just like Grace was now, only she was waiting on the snake.

All this time later, she was in the same alley, by the same dumpster, where she had saved Furby. Only this time, she was saving herself.

It wasn't long before the band began their exit through the door. She stayed still in the shadows, not wanting to attract their attention. She was there for one reason and one reason only.

They filed out through the alley. Brent was last.

When she called out his name, he turned.

"Well, well, well, what do we have here?" he said, his grin fake and malicious. His blue eyes piercing in the dim light. "Slumming are you, Grace? Or did you just want another night with me?"

"Well, Brent, the last time seemed to leave my memory somewhat....lacking. Perhaps it wasn't really all that mind blowing."

He stiffened on that one, "You've always been a bitch, you know that? What are you here for now? To rub your tour in my face? Your one-hit wonder song?"

"Three songs, Brent. We had three songs hit the charts. I think I owe a little bit of that success to you. If it hadn't been for you, I'd have never left New Orleans. I'd still be playing the same set of songs in the same bar. Just like you. You're mediocre, Brent, and this is all you are ever going to be. You never wanted me to sing those songs with your band. Always had to be in control. It could have been you on tour. But, it wasn't. It was me. And I loved every single minute of it."

She paused for a moment and smiled, "You will *never* know how that feels. How success feels. I win, Brent. I win."

Finished, she shook her head at him, looking him in the eye then shaking her head. She brushed past him leaving him standing alone in the alley.

As she walked back to the hotel, she pulled out the cigarette and lit it. *Ivy was right, a smoke does taste good after exorcizing old ghosts.*

CHRISTMAS EVE

Back at the Redbird Inn, Grace woke up and quietly got out of bed, not wanting to wake Gabriel up. The sun was just barely starting to rise and Grace wanted to see the sunset over the water. She threw on a hoodie and some jogging pants and got ready for a walk.

Furby jumped up from his hiding spot nestled in some pillows, and bounced out of the bed to follow. She grabbed his leash from the dresser and headed for the kitchen.

She set the coffee pot to brew and gathered her shoes. After Furby was leashed they set off down the beach.

It was just the two of them. The only people that might be out this early would be Noah and his dogs. Noah loved his morning runs as much as Grace did.

She didn't feel like running though. She felt like she'd been running too long and too hard from something that relentless pursued her. She was done.

She let Furby off his leash, and he went to explore the edges of the surf. He would be wet and sandy and absolutely hate the bath he would have to suffer through later, but now, he was enjoying just being free.

They walked along the coast, Grace admiring the pinks and yellows of the water and the sky as she meandered along, lost in thought. She had not talked to Gabe yet about her run-in with Brent, but she would. For now, she was enjoying simply being with him. They had spent the morning after the ball in the French Quarter, holding hands and stealing kisses as they wandered in and out of the hotels enjoying the grand Christmas decorations. It was a new beginning. Her wounds were healing as was their relationship.

She walked until she was across from the old Snapper's. She whistled at Furby then, and he followed her to the bare concrete slab that used to be an old bait shop, and then a bar and grill. She took a seat on a piece of concrete rubble and looked around. This needed to be rebuilt. It had been a fixture in this town for too long. She understood Carly's need for change. Too well, as Grace had needed her own.

As she was thinking, she watched Noah run by with his dog Sadie, who had become his support dog. It had done wonders for him. He wasn't as uneasy in groups, he wasn't as withdrawn, and wasn't near as tense.

It was amazing what a dog could do to help heal a human. Furby had definitely played a part in her own journey.

It was then an idea began to take root. She reached in her pocket and pulled out the skeleton key she had bought at *Enchantee*. New doors. New beginnings.

She was still sitting there an hour later, when Gabe walked up. Furby ran to meet him, and he picked the little dog up and snuggled him close. He smiled as he wrapped Grace in his arms.

"Merry Christmas Eve," he said, placing a kiss on her forehead. "We need some mistletoe."

She looked up, "Nowhere to hang it here."

"I guess you're right about that."

"But you don't need mistletoe to kiss me."

He put Furby down, pulled her close, and lowered his face to hers. Kissing her slowly, and tenderly, it sent tremors through her body and made her knees weak. She pulled back, and took his hand.

"I have an idea."

"Oh yeah, what's that?"

"I was thinking that I would like to rebuild Snapper's. Bon Chance could use a music venue. It would be more about music though than a bar and grill. Or the bait shop it had been before. We could have a great stage and equipment. I was thinking that we could even do a charity festival once a year. We know enough musicians to get a line-up."

Gabriel's green eyes lit up, "Oh yeah, and what charity were you thinking?"

"Something for support dogs. Maybe some program that helps train the dogs, or something? I'd have to do some research."

"And what about touring?"

"We could still tour. We could just hire good people to hold the fort here while we are out on the road. I'm sure the people who worked for Carly would be interested in coming back. And we have down time between tours."

"I think it's a great idea. And I love the festival idea. What a great idea to bring more business to Bon Chance."

"Exactly. I'd have to talk to Carly, but I'm sure she'd be on board with selling. Plus, she loves music, so this would be right up her alley."

"We can talk to her together. I'm in this with you. Let's do it."

She grinned and threw herself in his arms. "Yes!"

Furby, sensing their excitement, danced happily around their legs.

"Merry Christmas, Gabe."

"Merry Christmas, Grace."

About the Author

A.L. Vincent is a teacher/writer who lives in the heart of Cajun Country. Born in Oklahoma, Vincent became fascinated with South Louisiana after reading Interview With the Vampire. Finally, she became a Cajun transplant in 2001. When not getting lost in a story line, Vincent can be found cooking or enjoying live local music. You can read more of Grace and Gabe's story in *Running on Empty*, the second book in the Boonie series.

Social Media Links:

Reader's Group: https://www.facebook.com/groups/425463904324654/

Instagram: https://instagram.com/lishaleigh75

Newsletter: http://eepurl.com/bRiinr

Facebook: https://www.facebook.com/ALVincentAuthor/

Twitter: https://twitter.com/soonergirl1975

BookBub: https://www.bookbub.com/profile/a-l-vincent

Amazon: https://www.amazon.com/-/e/B016X3YYW2

COMMUNITY. COURAGE. Compassion.

Hometown Heroes brings you five Christmas romances that celebrate everyday heroes.

From paranormal to contemporary to historical, there's something here to fill everyone with the spirit of the season.

A portion of the proceeds will be donated to Cajun Navy Relief, an organization dedicated to helping neighbors in distress.

Amazon Buy Link: https://amzn.to/2vfDg8y

BIENVENUE PRESS

About the Publisher

Bienvenue Press opened its doors in June 2017. While our initial focus is on Southern fiction, we hope to branch out into other genres in the future as we continue to grow. In order to help our authors make their books the best they can be, we plan to publish six books in our inaugural year.

Our staff has years of combined experience in the writing and editing world. We are teachers, writers, journalists, and readers. We have a deep love for words, writing, and books.

Join our reader's group to stay updated on new releases! https://bit.ly/2OFOM46